War Comes
to Willy Freeman

War Comes
to Willy Freeman

James Lincoln Collier • Christopher Collier

DELACORTE PRESS/NEW YORK

Published by
Delacorte Press
1 Dag Hammarskjold Plaza
New York, N.Y. 10017

Manufactured in the United States of America

9 8 7 6 5 4

LIBRARY OF CONGRESS CATALOGING IN PUBLICATION DATA

Collier, James Lincoln [date of birth]
War comes to Willy Freeman.

Summary: A free thirteen-year-old black
girl in Connecticut is caught up in the horror
of the Revolutionary War and the danger of being
returned to slavery when her patriot father
is killed by the British and her mother disappears.
[1.   United States—History—Revolution,
1775–1783—Fiction.   2. Afro-Americans—
Fiction.   3. Slavery—Fiction.]   I. Collier,
Christopher.   II. Title.
PZ7.C678War   1983   [Fic]   82-70317
ISBN 0-385-29235-X   AACR2

for
Catherine Bromberger

1

WHAT I REMEMBERED most was the way the sun flashed and flashed on the bayonets. The British soldiers marched past our cabin in their red jackets, raising dust from the road, and the bayonets flashed and flashed, now this one, now the next one, as they turned just so in the morning sun. Oh, it scared me something awful, knowing that before too long they would march up to Fort Griswold and try to run them bayonets through a lot of our people, and maybe Pa, too, if they hadn't caught him already.

"Ma, I'm scared for Pa," I said.

"Hush now, my honey," she said. "Your Pa'll be all right."

She was just saying that. Ma, she didn't like for me to be unhappy, and she was just saying that so's I wouldn't worry. We stood side by side in front of our little wooden cabin, the September sun still warm on our skin, smelling the dust raised up by the marching men dry in our noses. Their feet went clap clap clap on the ground, and the drums rolled, and the bayonets flashed. Sometimes a soldier would give us a quick look as we stood there, but mostly they just marched on, staring straight ahead in the dusty sunlight.

"I wish Pa was here," I said.

"Just as good he ain't," Ma said. "He's bound and determined to fight. I'd rather he was out there on the water fishing than chasing up to Fort Griswold to get himself stuck with one of them bayonets."

"Will he really fight?" I said. But I knew he would. He was mighty brave. I'd seen him go out on Long Island Sound in the jolly boat when it was storming so fierce you could hardly stand up. There was nothing Pa was afraid of.

"Oh, he'll fight all right," Ma said. "He'll fight. I told him until my jaws ached that there wasn't no use in us niggers fighting, we wasn't going to get anything out of it no matter who wins. But he says no, we're free now, and it's our country, too."

She looked mighty grim and bitter, like there wasn't nothing fair in anything. Pa'd got his freedom from Colonel Ledyard by joining up in the militia. That was the law—if a black slave was going to join up to fight the British, he had to be set free first. So Pa joined up, and then Colonel Ledyard gave me and Ma our freedom, too. Pa took the name of Freeman, so he was

2

Jordan Freeman, and Ma was Lucy Freeman, and I was Wilhelmina Freeman. It was kind of a funny feeling having a last name all of a sudden, after nine years of not having one. But now I was thirteen and I'd got used to it. Besides, nobody called me nothing but Willy, anyway.

So the soldiers went marching past, raising up the dust, and I watched, wondering if one of those bayonets would go into Pa. Finally Ma said, "Willy, war or no war, the cow ain't going to milk herself. You go along now."

The cow was Ma's. Mrs. Ledyard had given it to her once when she'd nursed the Ledyards' little girl through the fever, when nobody thought she would live. Ma was mighty careful about that cow. We had a horse, too, down in the salt marsh, but it belonged to Colonel Ledyard.

We lived out on a little spit of land that bordered on the Thames River, where it ran into Long Island Sound. There was a salt marsh on the water side. On the inland side the land rose up into hills, with oaks and pines on them. Further up the Thames was the village of Groton, where Fort Griswold was. On the other side of the Thames was New London. It was a mighty big place, with docks sticking into the river, and hundreds of houses and six church steeples you could count if you went up into the hills.

I went into the house, got the wooden milk bucket, and came out again. Ma took a look at me. "Put on them milking britches, Willy," she said. "I ain't having

3

no child of mine sitting on a milking stool with her skirt pulled up, and all them soldiers marching by."

That was Ma—she didn't hold with anybody seeing a girl's legs. I didn't care one way or another, I just hated changing my clothes all the time, because I'd have to change back into my dress soon as the milking was done—naturally, Ma didn't hold with a girl going around dressed up like a boy, neither. "Ma—" I started to argue.

She gave me a look. "You do like I say, Willy."

I might have argued, too, but I was feeling terrible scared by the British, and I didn't have much mind for arguing like mostly I would. So I went into the cabin and put on the milking britches, and then I went down to the salt marsh behind the cabin and started to milk the cow, while the horse stood near and watched.

I'd just got started when there was a great boom from somewhere behind me. I jumped. Then there was a tearing sound overhead, and I knew they'd begun to fire cannon from Fort Griswold out onto the British ships.

That cannon ball tearing out to sea scared me even more, because Pa was out there somewhere in the jolly boat. If a ball struck the boat, it would smash it to smithereens and drown Pa for sure. Oh, how I wished he was back home with us, never mind what Ma said.

Mostly Pa worked for Colonel Ledyard, chopping wood, hoeing corn, and running and fetching. But early in the mornings he went out fishing, so as to make a little money to improve himself. I thought about him out there amongst the British fleet and I wondered if he was scared. Then I began to think about if he would really fight, the way Ma said, and what that would be like. What would it be like to get stabbed by a bayonet?

Thinking about that scared me so much I had to squinch my eyes closed and think about milking the cow. By and by I was finished, and I left the cow on her tether and carried the milk bucket up to the cabin. There was cannons rolling past now, and the dust was worse than ever. Just as I got to the door there came another boom and the tearing noise overhead. I jumped inside and shut the door, even though I knew if a ball hit, it would go clean through the cabin, door and all. 'Course, there wasn't much to our cabin—just a rope bed with a corn shuck mattress for Ma and Pa and a pallet for me, and a pine table and a cupboard and the fireplace and such.

Ma was fixing some cold pork and biscuits for breakfast. I said, "How am I going to get the milk up to Colonel Ledyard's, Ma?" We sold our extra milk to Colonel Ledyard, and most mornings I rode up there on the horse with it. I'd done it for years. I could ride pretty good. I wasn't supposed to race the horse, but sometimes I did anyway, when nobody was looking.

Ma went to the window and looked out at the troops marching through the hazy sunshine. "Colonel Ledyard will have to wait for his milk," she said. "I reckon he's got other things on his mind this morning."

But the troops was making just an awful noise. The

cannon wheels was rumbling, the axles squeaking, and the drums rat-tat-tatting; still we didn't have no trouble hearing the cannons up at Fort Griswold booming and the balls whistling overhead. I stood by the window, staring out, scared and wondering how our militia could ever stand up to them men and cannons going by.

Ma put the piece of cold pork and a plate of biscuits on the table. "No reason for us not to eat breakfast," she said. "You got to feed yourself, war or no war." I sat down. I didn't much feel like eating, but I chewed some biscuit anyway, because I knew I'd better keep my strength up for whatever happened that day. And just about the time I was washing the biscuit down with a swallow of beer, the rumbling and squeaking of the cannon began to die down, and the drums to fade off. I jumped up and went to the door.

The air was still filled with the brown dust drifting up everywhere and a few men was straggling through it. As I stood there a horseman galloped up and sped by; and then they was all disappearing through the dust down the road toward Fort Griswold.

"They're gone, Ma," I said.

"Not far," she said. "Not far enough."

I turned away from the door and looked at her. I'd never seen her so terrible grim before, her eyes hard as steel, her lips clenched tight. She was pretty, Ma was, with chocolate-colored skin and hair cut short like mine, and I hoped I'd be as pretty as her when I was grown. But she didn't look pretty right then.

6

"Maybe the militia won't fight, Ma," I said. "Maybe they'll just give up when they see all them British."

"They'll fight," she said. "There'll be plenty dead before night."

Then a shrill, high scream cut like a knife through the air. We jumped up. "The cow," Ma cried.

We dashed out of the cabin into the sunlight hazy with dust. There were two soldiers down in the salt marsh. The cow was collapsed down on her side, kicking her legs and trying to stand up. The soldiers stabbed with their bayonets. The cow shrieked again, and tried to roll up onto her feet.

"Stop, for the love of God, stop," Ma cried. She began to run, and I ran after her.

The soldiers turned, and I saw a funny thing: they was black. They watched us run up.

"Stop, please stop," Ma cried.

We came up to them. The cow was gasping for breath and there was foamy blood all over her mouth and nose and I knew she was dying. She rolled her eyes up to look at us, like she couldn't understand what was happening to her.

"For God's sake, why are you doing this?" Ma shouted.

The two soldiers looked uneasy. "If we'd known you was niggers, we'd have left the cow alone," one of them said. "We ain't supposed to bother the black folk."

Ma dropped down on her knees by the cow. Now I saw a big cut in her side where they'd run her through.

7

"You've killed her," Ma said. Her voice was flat and her eyes hard as steel again, like she wasn't going to let nothing bother her, no matter what. She stood up and looked at the soldiers with that flat, steely look. "You've killed her. She was mine. She was the only thing I ever owned."

"If we'd known you was—"

"The cabin ain't mine, the boat ain't mine, the clothes on my back ain't mine, but Mrs. Ledyard, she said, 'Lucy, take the cow, it's yours, a woman ought to have something that's her own.' " Then Ma did something I never heard her do before. She cursed. "God damn you to hell," she said. "You killed her, now take her."

She turned around and walked off across the salt marsh to the cabin, and I followed after her. We got inside. She stood by the window, staring out at the haze, but I knew she wasn't seeing it, she was seeing something inside her head. I didn't know what, but she was so grim-looking I didn't dare speak. Then suddenly she got soft again. She came away from the window, knelt down in front of me, and put her arms around me. "Oh, my honey," she said, "I shouldn't talk like that. Your Pa, he's a good man. He's always done right by us and don't drink and carry on like some. But there ain't much a woman can have for herself, and it hurts mighty awful to lose what little you got."

But I was thinking about something else. "Ma, was them soldiers right when they said they wasn't suppose to bother black folks?"

She sighed and stood up. "I reckon so," she said. "The British generals figure if they don't treat us too hard we'll come onto their side. Some black folks say there ain't much sense in fighting for the Americans when most likely they'll keep black folks slaves if they win."

"Pa don't feel that way."

"No, your Pa, he's made his mind up he's an American by law and right and he's going to fight for it. Why do you think he's up drilling with Colonel Ledyard's militia all the time? There's your uncle Jack, too, gone off to fight with General Washington years ago. Your aunt Betsy, she hardly sees him from one year to the next."

"But then he'll be free."

"If he ain't killed," Ma said. "And it won't do Betsy much good, nor your cousin Daniel, neither, because they'll still be slaves, no matter what."

"But you said that Uncle Jack will buy them free."

"If he lives and gets his soldier's pay, and they don't get sold off to the West Indies first."

I knew all about that. After Colonel Ledyard set us free, Ma took a trip down the coast to Stratford to visit Aunt Betsy and Uncle Jack and my little cousin Dan. They was slaves of Captain Ivers. When she came back, she told us about Uncle Jack going off to fight. If he saved up his pay, Ma said, he'd maybe have enough money to buy Aunt Betsy and Cousin Dan free, too. But like Ma said, it wouldn't be no use if he got killed first.

9

And I was thinking it wouldn't be no use for Pa to be free if he got himself killed, neither, when suddenly there was a knock on the cabin door. Ma went and opened it a little, cautious. It was the two black soldiers. I noticed their uniforms was different; they had no leggins, short jackets, and no white straps across their chests. One of them was carrying a haunch of the cow, and the other had a bucket. "Here," he said. "If we'd known you was black we wouldn't have touched the cow."

Ma gave him that cold look. "I don't want it. You killed her, take it."

I knew I should be quiet and not get into trouble, but I was curious and couldn't help myself. "I didn't know niggers was British," I said.

"We ain't British. We're from New Jersey. The Third New Jersey Volunteers."

"Why are you fighting for the British?" I said.

"Why are you rebels?" the soldier said. "What's the use in fighting for the Americans when they're just going to keep you slaves?"

"We're not slaves," I said. "We're free."

"Keep your mouth shut, Willy," Ma said.

"You know what you ought to do, missus," the soldier said to Ma. "You ought to take the boy down to the boats and go back to New York with us." I forgot I looked like a boy in the britches.

Ma cocked her head. "We hear a lot of black folks that joined up with the British got sold off to the West Indies."

"That's just stories," the soldier said.

"Maybe," Ma said.

"I'm giving you good advice. Go off with us. There won't be much left around here anyways when we get finished today."

That made me go cold, for Pa would have to fight, if he wasn't dead already. "What are you coming up here to make trouble for?" I said.

"Hush up, my honey," Ma said.

She shouldn't have said it. The soldier leaned forward and looked hard into my face. "Are you a boy or a girl?" he asked.

I began to blush. "Can't you tell?"

"He's a boy," Ma said.

The soldier went on staring into my face. "I don't believe it," he said. Suddenly he reached his hand out to my shirt and felt for my breasts. "I figured you was a girl," he said. It gave me a queer, dirty feeling to have him mess with my body like that.

And just then Pa stepped up behind them. He had a log in his hands. My heart jumped. "Take your hands off that child," he said calmly, "or I'm going to kill you."

2

THE SOLDIER WHO WAS touching me swiveled around to look at Pa, but he didn't take his hand away.

"I told you to take your hand off that child," he said again.

The soldier let go of me and laughed. I kind of jumped back into the cabin door. The soldier raised up his musket and poked the bayonet toward Pa. "You're going to do what?" he said.

"If you touch her again, I'll tear your head off," Pa said, still in that calm way.

He stared at the soldier and the soldier stared back, and for a minute they stood like that. Nobody moved. Finally the soldier said, "If you was white, I'd run you through."

Pa didn't say anything. He just went on staring,

holding the log with both hands over his shoulder. Then the other soldier said, "Never mind this. Let's get the water." The first soldier didn't move, but went on staring at Pa. "Come on," the other one said. "We're going to catch it from the lieutenant if we don't get back soon with some water." He grabbed the first soldier's arm and shook it.

The first soldier spit into the dirt in front of the cabin. "You're lucky," he said to Pa. "If you'd been white, I'd run you through." He turned and strode off, the other one coming after him, the bucket handle creaking in its sockets.

We watched them go off for a minute. Then Pa said, "Is the horse all right?"

"Yes," Ma said. "They got the cow, but they never saw the horse."

"Good," he said. Suddenly we heard a fast pop-pop-pop from across the river. They were fighting in New London already. "I've got to get up to Fort Griswold."

"Jordan—" Ma started. Her eyes looked hurt and sad.

"Get me something to eat, Lucy," Pa said.

"Jordan, please, you have a child."

He pushed past her into the cabin. "Don't be arguing with me, Lucy," he said. Pa didn't like no arguing. Sometimes I'd just open my mouth and he'd tell me not to be argumentative. "Get me something to eat."

Ma went into the cabin behind him and I came after her. Pa sat down at the plank table, and Ma got out

14

the pork and biscuits and put it on a plate in front of him. She wanted to argue with him, but she didn't dare. He was the man, and she had to do what he told her to do. She was hurting inside, I could see that pretty clear.

I figured Pa knew it, too, but he sat there like he didn't know. While he ate, he told us what had happened. He'd gone out as usual to get the jolly boat and go fishing, but the minute he got down to the beach where he kept the boat pulled up on the sand he'd seen the British fleet standing offshore about three miles. They were beating back and forth, and from the distance he hadn't been able to tell whether they were coming into New London or not. He knew right away he ought to find out, so's to warn people if the ships were headed for us. So he'd pushed the jolly into the water, jumped in, hoisted sail, and went on out. It was a risky thing to do, because it would be pretty clear to the British that a lone fishing boat sailing around them was spying on them. But that was the way Pa was—he wasn't afraid of anything.

He had the wind at his back, and it didn't take him more than fifteen or twenty minutes to get close enough to see that the fleet was driving for New London. He came about to head back and raise the alarm, but now he had the wind against him. Just about then the British spotted him. They began shooting at him with muskets, but he was too far away, and them muskets wasn't very good at that range. So they let go at him with a cannon. Tacking back and forth across the wind the way he had to, he was going to be in cannon range a long time, so he turned and started east up the coast. On a reach across the wind like that he could make pretty good time. The British kept flinging cannonballs after him, trying to smash the boat, or at least tear out the sail. They came mighty close to doing it, too. A couple of times he saw the balls skip off the water right alongside the boat. But they never got him, and by and by he was out of range and they gave up.

But now he was way up the coast, six or seven miles from home, near a place called Long Point. He angled into shore, came about, and headed back, keeping as close to shore as he could, so's the sail would blend in with the white sand of the beach. But he didn't dare come all the way in. He turned into Baker's Cove a couple of miles to the east of Groton Point. He tied the boat up there to a tree where nobody was likely to see it. Then he crept up into the woods and waited there until the British got finished marching past. As he was coming back down he saw the two soldiers talking to us, and he picked up the log: he figured they were up to no good and he wanted to be ready. It was pretty foolish, just a log against a couple of men with guns and bayonets, but that was the way Pa was. If that soldier hadn't taken his hand off me, Pa would have whacked him one with the log, that was for sure.

The muskets kept popping away in New London

16

across the river, and there was sounds of firing from Fort Griswold now, too. Out the window we could see smoke rising up from someplace and drifting around in the air. There were faint, distant shouts, too.

Pa jumped up. "I've got to go," he said. "I've got to get to the fort before the British get up there."

Suddenly I realized that Ma was standing in the doorway. Her two hands were clenched together and she wasn't moving. She stared at Pa. "Jordan, please—"

"Lucy, get out of my way," he said.

Then she dropped down on her knees. "I'm begging you, Jordan." Her eyes were hurt and sick, and I knew how much she hated begging him. But she went on kneeling there. "Please, Jordan."

He looked away to me. "Willy, I want you to ride up there with me to bring the horse back."

"Not the child," Ma cried. "You'll get her killed."

"I ain't going to get her killed," he said in his calm voice.

She jumped up. "Don't go, Willy," she cried.

"She'll do what she's told," Pa said.

"She's just a child, Jordan."

"No, she ain't. She's thirteen."

"She's a girl, she's not a man."

That stopped him for a minute. He stood looking at me. Then he said, "Willy, get one of my cockade hats out of the cupboard. With them britches on, you look like a boy, anyway."

So I got his cockade hat—it was brown, with a

yellow ribbon—and put it on. Pa looked me over. Then he pushed past Ma through the door and I went with him. I didn't dare go against him.

He brought the horse around the cabin and I climbed up behind him. There wasn't any going against him; he was the man. I sort of wanted to go, anyway. I wanted to see what it was like. But I was mighty scared, too. As we rode away up the road I turned to look back at Ma. She was standing in the doorway with her hands over her face, all bent over. I waved, but the way she had her face covered she couldn't see me.

We went on up the road a ways. All along there was people running, carrying stuff in their arms or slung over their backs—taking boxes and bags and chairs or pictures into the fields and woods to hide them from the British. Crazy old Granny Hyde was leading a piglet along on a string.

Fort Griswold was up ahead on a steep slope off the road. There was plenty of popping coming from up there, and sometimes the big boom of a cannon. We went on until we was about a mile or so from the fort, and then Pa turned the horse off into woods, so's we could circle around and come up to the fort from behind. The woods rose up and when we got a little higher I could see New London across the Thames. There was smoke drifting up out of it now, and there was flames and black smoke boiling up on the dock. The British was going to burn the town down, I knew that. They'd done it to plenty of other towns, like

18

Danbury, over in the western part of Connecticut, and New Haven and Fairfield and Norwalk right along Long Island Sound. I wondered if they'd burn Groton down, too.

Now we began to circle back toward the fort. The firing kept getting louder and louder. Each time a musket cracked I jumped and closed my eyes. The gunsmoke was drifting through the trees like thin ghosts. I was scared pretty good by now, and I wished Pa would change his mind and turn around and go home. Or maybe we'd get up there and find the fort surrounded by the British and no way to get in. But he just kept pushing forward.

Then ahead the woods began to thin out and the smoke got thicker. My heart began to race and my legs felt weak and wobbly. We climbed down off the horse, and Pa tied her to a tree. We crept forward on our hands and knees to the edge of the woods.

Fort Griswold was dead ahead of us. It was made of stone, maybe nine feet high. They'd piled dirt partway up the stone. On top of the stone walls was a plank fence, sticking out at an angle to make it hard to climb over. A couple of cannon stuck out through gaps in the boards. I could see the heads of men and muskets and bayonets.

The British were off to the left on the downslope, lying behind rocks and little ridges in the ground, firing up at the fort. Some of the New Jersey soldiers with bare legs were pushing cannons up the slope. I looked at Pa, lying beside me. He was looking at the

19

British and then over to the fort and back to the British again, calculating. Then he turned to me. "Willy, I'm going to make a run for it round the north side. There's no one shooting from there yet, and once I'm up against the walls the British won't be able to get a clean shot at me, anyway."

"How are you going to get over them walls, Pa?"

"Somebody up top is bound to see me," he said. "They'll give me a hand up." He took another look down the slope to the British. Then he turned back to me. "Now, you wait here until you see me safe into the fort, just in case I can't make it. Once I'm up in there, you get on the horse and run on home to your Ma. Understand?"

"Yes, Pa," I said.

He put his arm around my shoulders to give me a quick hug and kissed me on the forehead. "You be a brave girl now, and help your Ma all you can."

"Yes, Pa," I said. A shiver passed through me, because I knew he was likely to be killed up there in the fort.

Then he jumped up onto his feet and, crouching low, began to run across the open space to the fort. I looked down at the British. They spotted him right away. They swiveled around and let go at him. My heart was pounding. "Oh, run, Pa," I said aloud. He went running crouched over and in a moment he was up against the wall of the fort, looking up, hollering and waving. He wasn't there more than five seconds before they let down a rope. He grabbed onto it and they pulled him up headfirst over the wall. I wondered if those legs disappearing over the wall was the last I'd ever see of him.

Now I turned and crawled back through the woods to where the horse was tied to a tree. She was prancing around and snapping her head up and down, and I knew she was as scared as I was of the noise and the smoke ghosts drifting through the woods. I patted her a couple of times to calm her down a little. Then I untied her and climbed up on her, and that was when I saw a whole bunch of red jackets come through the woods smack toward me.

I jerked on the reins to swing the horse around so as to circle past them in the woods, but they saw me. "Spy, spy," I heard one of them shout, and then I heard a bang just behind me again. I kicked the horse, and the next thing I knew I was charging out of the woods into the open space toward the fort. I hunched down on the horse's back, hanging on to her neck, trying to push myself right down into her skin. My eyes was closed and all I could think was that any second a musket ball could catch me in the back.

3

I FELT WEAK AND COLD and my heart was pounding so hard I could hear it racing in my head over the noise of the fighting. It seemed like I was galloping across the clearing for hours. I opened my eyes. The fort was dead ahead, twenty-five yards away. I kicked the horse again, and we came up to the wall. Just as I slid off her back, she shrieked and rose up on her hind legs, and I knew she'd taken a musket ball somewhere. I reached out to pat her, but she broke and ran, and then I felt something hit my shoulder. It was a rope. I grabbed it and looked up. There was Pa, looking down over the wall, and then I began to rise up, keeping my head turned away toward the wall, so's at least I wouldn't catch a ball in my face. Something snapped against the stones of the wall, flinging tiny bits of rock into my face. The bits of rock stung, and some got into my mouth. I spit, and then Pa was pulling me over the wooden palisades into the fort and I was safe.

I was up on a kind of wood platform that ran all the way around the inside of the fort about four feet below the top of the palisades. There were men crouched all along here, firing out at the British. There was cannons at the corners, with three or four men on each. Down in the center of the fort there was a well and a low wooden shed that I figured was a barracks for the soldiers to be in when they wasn't fighting. Underneath the platform there was a little room where they stored the gun powder and balls and such.

In the middle of the fort, next to the well, there was four men stretched out. I stared at them. One of them was moving his legs slowly back and forth and holding his side. He was pale and breathing hard. I didn't know if he was dying or not, but he was suffering something awful. The other three wasn't moving at all. They just lay on their backs and stared up at the sky.

All at once the shooting began to die off, and in a minute it stopped altogether. The silence was queer. The men began to talk and look over the wall, and Pa and I looked over the wall, too. We saw three British officers walking slowly up the slope to the fort, carrying a white flag. On a platform across the fort from us I saw Colonel Ledyard, with some men clustered around him. Suddenly one of the men raised his musket and fired. I looked out. The three British officers had stopped walking and were standing in the dusty ground, still holding the white flag. Then three of the men who had been with Colonel Ledyard climbed down from the platform, went out the door to the fort, and down the slope to talk to the British. In a couple of minutes they came back and climbed back up onto the platform to report to Colonel Ledyard.

"I'm going to find out what's happening," Pa said. He worked his way along the platform, stopping to talk with the men here and there, and in a moment he came back. "The British want us to surrender," he said. "We ain't going to. We're going to fight." He looked pretty serious. "They threaten to massacre us if we don't surrender."

"Will they, Pa?"

"No," he said. "It's just threats." He looked out over the palisade. "I wish you wasn't in here to see this, Willy." He went on looking around outside the fort. "I wish you could make a run for it, but it's too risky. They're moving around behind the fort now. The woods is full of them. There ain't any good way to get out."

"I'll be all right, Pa," I said. But I wasn't so sure I would. I couldn't keep my eyes off those men lying out there in the dirt—one of them still moving his legs slowly back and forth, and the others so still. There were flies on their faces now. My mouth was dry and my stomach began to turn over. I wished they would move, but they never did. I wondered if I would be able to stand it if I saw somebody get killed.

"Willy, go down into the powder magazine. You'll

be safer down there, and you can help them make cartridges."

I was glad enough to get away where I wouldn't see too much. I was curious, but I didn't know how much of it I could watch. Here and there was ladders going down from the platform. I climbed down one and trotted across the fort to the powder magazine, steering around the bodies with the flies on them. The magazine was just a little room. It was pretty dark in there, and they'd left the door open so's to get some light. There was boxes of balls and barrels of powder; you couldn't have any kind of lantern down there with all that powder around.

There was a white boy down there about my age. I knew who he was, too—William Latham. His Pa was Captain William Latham, and they lived in Groton. I went in. "My Pa says I'm to help," I said.

He gave me a funny look. He knew he knew me, but dressed up like a boy the way I was he couldn't figure me out. I was going to tell him, but then suddenly it came to me that if I told him I was a girl he'd start giving me orders and maybe wouldn't let me help with the cartridges. Of course me being black and him white he was likely to give me orders anyway, but not so much as if I was a girl. So I didn't say anything about who I was. "Are you making cartridges?"

He showed me how to do it. First he tore off a little square of some paper that was lying near him and wrapped it around a stick to make a tube. He twisted the bottom of the tube closed and took it off the stick.

Then he dropped in some powder and a ball, twisted the other end of the tube closed, and put the cartridge in a basket. All a soldier had to do was pour the powder down the barrel of his musket, drop the cartridge in and tap it home with the ramrod to make sure it was all the way down the barrel. Then he'd spill a bit of powder on the pan and fire. It saved an awful lot of time for the soldiers to have a pile of cartridges ready.

So I set to work, feeling mighty scared, and just about then the firing took up again. From down there in the magazine I could hear the cannonballs thudding against the wooden palisades, and men cursing and shouting and running along the platform overhead. Every few minutes the cannon would go off, shaking the whole fort. The sharp smell of gunsmoke drifted around everywhere. Oh, I was scared, just as scared as I could be, feeling cold and pale and trembly. I knelt next to William Latham, making cartridges and putting them in the basket.

"Do you think they'll break in?" I said.

He shook his head. His eyes was wide and he was as pale as I was. "They said they'd kill us all if we wouldn't surrender."

"Pa said that was just bluster."

He gave me a look. "Who's your Pa?"

"You don't know him," I said. "We're from over to New London."

He gave me another look, like he knew I was lying, but just then a soldier swung his head into the door and shouted, "Get some cartridges up there, quick."

I looked at William and he looked at me. "I'll go," he said. "You can go next time."

He picked up the basket and went out the door. I went on kneeling there, making cartridges, feeling sort of numb from the noise and shouts and the uproar. Out in the yard now there was a half dozen more men lying there, some of them just wounded and shaking and moaning, and some of them lying still. It kept worrying me that one of them might be Pa, but kneeling down that way I couldn't see them very well. I wondered if I ought to go out there and help the ones that was wounded, especially if one of them was Pa. They might need water, or to have their wounds tied up. But I reckoned it was more important to go on making cartridges.

Suddenly William dropped down from the platform in front of the door and jumped inside.

"What's happening?" I asked.

"Oh, it's mighty bad," he said. "The British are all around the fort, right up by the walls. They're trying to climb up, and there's a bunch of them at the door, hammering at it."

"Did you see my Pa?" I'd forgotten that he wasn't supposed to know who we was.

He gave me another funny look. "There's two or three niggers up there," he said. "I didn't see any dead ones."

"There's a lot of dead?"

"Lots," he said. "Leastwise there's a lot down. The

28

British are climbing up the palisades and we're fighting them with pikes."

Now it was all roaring and shouting and banging. I could hear hard thumping on the fort door, and the splintering of wood and shouts and shrieks. "Are they breaking down the palisades?"

"It's your turn to go up with the cartridges," he said.

Oh, how I wished I hadn't decided to be a boy. If he'd known I was a girl, he'd have never sent me up there. But I wasn't going to go back on it now. I wasn't going to let him see me be a coward. Pa would hate that if he knew. So I picked up the basket, ducked out the magazine door, and started up the nearest ladder to the platform. As soon as I got halfway up I could see a big gap in the wooden palisades where the British had ripped out a couple of planks.

There was two or three British in the gap, hanging on with one hand and jabbing around with their bayonets. And there was three or four Americans jabbing back at them with pikes. Pa was with them, and I climbed on up and dropped down the basket. I saw Pa ram his spear right into the stomach of a British soldier. The soldier grabbed at it with both hands. Just then there was a great splintering crash.

The main door to the fort was busted open, and the British flooded in. They poured into the fort, roaring and shouting, and flashing those shiny bayonets around. My heart was racing and I didn't hardly even

29

know what I was doing. I got into a corner of the palisades and crouched there. Down below, the Americans was running back across the fort to get away from the British, and the British was swirling among them with their bayonets, jabbing and jabbing. They was going to kill us all, just like they said.

I looked over at Pa. A stream of British were climbing through the gap in the palisades. Pa and the others was backing away down the platform, poking at the British with their pikes, but there was about ten British for the three of them, and I knew they couldn't last. I just crouched there, sick and shaking and so scared I couldn't move.

Then I saw Colonel Ledyard in the middle of the fort. There was a British officer there. Colonel Ledyard jumped up to him, holding his sword sideways with a hand at each end and waving it up and down. He was going to surrender, and I thanked God for it, so the awfulness would stop.

"Who commands here?" the British officer shouted.

"I did," Colonel Ledyard said, handing his sword forward. "But you do now, sir."

The British officer took the sword and then, without waiting one second, jabbed it into Colonel Ledyard's side so that it went all the way through him and came out the other side. Colonel Ledyard never even made a noise, but fell down into the dirt.

And suddenly there was some Americans there, and Pa was among them. Somebody rammed a pike through the British officer. I couldn't see who done it, whether it was Pa or somebody else, but the next thing I knew there was British soldiers all around him, and I saw a bayonet go through his back and he flung his arms out like so, and fell off the bayonet to the ground. I began to shriek. The shouting and the killing went on and on, and I crouched there on the platform with my eyes closed, crying and moaning and waiting to be killed.

4

I DON'T KNOW HOW long I crouched there with my eyes
closed and tears running down, and sort of gasping; it
seemed like forever. Then I felt the platform rattle
next to me. I opened my eyes. A British soldier was
standing over me, his musket pulled back with a
bloody bayonet pointing right at me. I shrieked and
flung myself up against the palisades and put my
hands out in front to ward off the bayonet. His eyes
were blue and his hair was blond, and he seemed
young even to me. It was queer that this man who was
going to kill me was an actual person, not some kind
of devil or madman. And I guess it was realizing that
he was a human being like me that let me open my
mouth and say, "Please don't kill me. I'm not a boy,
I'm a girl."

He had his musket half drawn back. He stopped and stared into my face for a moment. "Why, so you are," he said, looking surprised. "What are you doing in this?"

"I came up with my Pa." I started sobbing. "He's already dead."

He grabbed me by the shoulder, spun me around, and took hold of the collar of my shirt. "Out of here now." He sort of shoved me off the platform onto the ground, jumped down beside me, and grabbed my collar again. Then he began shoving me through the terrible place toward the door. There were bodies everywhere, and the blood so thick in places it made the ground slippery. Soldiers was lying on the ground writhing while the British rammed bayonets into them, so's some of them must have got killed a dozen times. I wanted to close my eyes, but I couldn't. And then I was out of the fort and running across the battlefield toward the woods as fast as I could go, sobbing so much that the tears flew off my face behind me as I ran.

There were soldiers all around on the hillside, some of the British regulars with white leggins and some of the New Jersey ones with bare legs, who we'd seen pushing the cannons up the rocky slope. They'd got a couple of the cannon up now, but there wasn't anybody left for them to kill.

As I ducked into the woods I could still hear shouts from up at the fort, and muskets banging away. But it had slowed down a lot, and I knew that they'd killed most of the American militia and didn't have anybody to shoot anymore. There was the smell of wood and molasses burning from New London across the river. I wondered if they was going to burn Groton, too. I thought about that, and what we'd do if they burned our cabin. I tried to think about the molasses burning so's not to think about Pa being stabbed by those bayonets.

The thing I wanted the most was to get home to Ma. I wanted to be with her so bad I could hardly stand it. I waited a few more minutes, and then I decided I was going home, British or no British.

I slipped down the hillside through the woods until I came to where the ground leveled out by the river. There was a little road here running along the shore. Smoke was boiling up from New London. It covered the river, but through it I could see boats being rowed hither and yon, and ships at the wharf burned to the waterline and another big ship afire drifting down the river. There was a few people going up the road to get away from Groton, women mostly, carrying bags and furniture and such, all looking mighty scared. Nobody paid any attention to me, so I began trotting along.

I was feeling odd, the queerest I'd ever felt in my life. My head was numb and I couldn't think straight about anything: ideas just came and went with no order nor reason. Down inside me was an awful pain. Try as I might not to, I kept seeing Pa with that bayonet going into his back and his arms flung out so. And all I knew was that I wanted my Ma in the worst way.

I trotted along, dazed, the only one going toward the beach; all the others were running north, trying to get away from the British. Once I passed a wagon with some men lying in the back of it all bloody, and I knew the British was bringing the wounded out of the fort. I wondered if Pa was still up there, and I hurried along to get home to Ma to tell her what had happened.

As I got along down toward our cabin, I could see out in the ocean the British fleet, standing at anchor, as calm as you please. Finally our cabin came in sight. It was sitting there in the afternoon sun just the way it had been in the morning when I'd left with Pa. It was just the same, but everything else was changed, and nothing would ever be the same again.

When I got to within a little ways of it, I began to run. I just wanted to throw my arms around Ma and hug her and have her hold me tight. I ran up to the door. It was open. I looked in. Nobody was there. Where was she? Why wasn't she waiting for me? "Ma?" I called out. "Ma, where are you?"

I looked around. Her bonnet and her cloak was hanging on the hook by the door where they always was. I went back outside and walked around the cabin, looking off in the distance for her and shouting "Ma, Ma" over and over; but I didn't get nothing back. Tears began to run down my cheeks again. I went back into the cabin to see if there was any signs of where she'd gone. I figured maybe she'd hidden some stuff out in the woods like the rest, and was out there collecting it back. Oh, there were a lot of places she could have gone. She could even have gone up to the fort looking for me and Pa.

I sat on the ground by the roadside with my back up against the cabin wall so I'd see Ma when she was heading home. I sat there for a long time, trying not to cry, but gasping sometimes and wiping tears away. The sun was way out to the west, dropping down behind New London lighthouse, and the woods was filled with shadows. A little evening breeze came up off the water. With the sun going down it was getting chilly. I shivered. Where was Ma? Had the British got her? Had they done something to her and flung her away someplace?

So I went on sitting there, watching the night come up and wondering what I ought to do. And just when I was thinking that maybe I should go up to Groton and look for her, I saw somebody coming down the road toward me. I waited and watched, praying that it would be Ma. But it wasn't; it was the old darkie named Granny Hyde. She lived alone in a little hut in the village and was always talking to herself, sort of crazy-like. She still had her pig tugging on a line behind her. She came up to me and stopped and stared at me. Then she said, "We thought you was dead, Willy. We thought you was dead for sure."

"Pa's dead," I said. "I saw it happen. They ran him

through with their bayonets. They killed most near everybody."

"I know," she said. "We thought you was dead, too, Willy."

"Where's Ma?"

She shook her head. "Gone."

"Gone?"

"Gone," she said. "The British took her. They took three or four niggers, heaved them into their boats and took them off to New York with them." She shook her head. "We won't see none of them ever again."

I couldn't believe it. I didn't want to believe it. What would I do with Pa dead and Ma captured? It gave me such a hopeless feeling, like all the air just went out of my stomach. The tears were running down my cheeks in rivers, it seemed like, and run into my mouth all salty. Try as I might to stop, I was sobbing again. Granny Hyde put her arm around my shoulders. "You go get your things, Willy," she said. "You come stay with me. I've got to go along now. You come soon." She went off with her pig along behind.

I didn't know what to do. I couldn't believe that Ma was really gone. I went back into the cabin. I was dead tired and I didn't feel like eating nothing, but I was thirsty and I drank a pot of beer. Then I took Ma's cloak down, lay on the bed with it wrapped around me, so's I could smell her smell. I just lay there sobbing and heaving and after a while I must have just fallen asleep.

When I woke up, the morning sky was getting gray

and the birds was chirping. It took me a minute to come to myself and remember what had happened. I sat up and said "Ma?" and looked around the cabin. She wasn't there. I busted out crying again. Where was she? Finally I realized that I couldn't go on crying forever, I had to do something, so I wiped my face on my sleeve, got up off the bed, and ate the rest of the biscuits that was there. Then I went out of the cabin and had a look around. It was gray dawn, but the sky was clear and it was going to be another sunny day. There was still smoke in the air drifting over from New London, with that burned molasses smell to it.

I didn't know if the British was gone or not. I knew I would be able to see out into the water from the hill that rose up toward Groton, so I walked up there through the woods, smelling the oaks and hemlocks. When I was far enough up, I looked out to sea. The British fleet was there, more ships than I'd ever seen in my life. There was a lot of transports, and among them great three-masted frigates with rows and rows of cannons along their sides and the British flag hanging limp in the light breeze. They was so close I could see the sailors scurrying around the decks. Oh, my, it scared me all over again to see those ships. They was like death itself.

I looked in the other direction, toward New London. It was mostly just ashes and chimneys, with columns of smoke coming up here and there. The wharves was all burned right down to the water, and there was a lot of hulls drifting around the harbor, burned down to the waterline, too. It was surprising to see a town just gone like that—there one morning and gone the next. It was like seeing half a person—just a pair of legs walking around with nothing above its belt.

All that really mattered to me, though, was that Pa was dead and Ma was gone. I was so numb from that that I could hardly think about anything else. But I had to get hold of myself and figure out what to do next. One thing I knew was that I wasn't going to go live with crazy old Granny Hyde.

I went back down to the cabin and sat at the plank table and thought about it. The question that come to me was how was I going to live. Colonel Ledyard, he was dead, so there wasn't any hope of working for him. Of course, Mrs. Ledyard, she might need help and maybe would take me on. But that wouldn't be no different from going back into slavery again. Mrs. Ledyard, she was going to be poor now and wouldn't be able to pay me nothing, just room and keep. The only way I'd ever get out of that would be to get married. But there wasn't hardly any black men left around, and none that I wanted to marry, anyway.

What I wanted most of all was to have Ma back. I missed her so, I felt all hollow in my stomach, and sometimes I missed her so much I just sort of gasped for breath.

But she was gone, and what could I do? Who was there for me? What relatives did I have? Only Aunt Betsy and Uncle Jack Arabus, and Cousin Dan, and

I'd never met any of them. Would they take me in? Ma always said how much she and Aunt Betsy loved each other. She was bound to take me in. I was kin. And right then I resolved that's what I'd do—I'd go down to Stratford to Aunt Betsy. She'd take me in.

Just thinking about it made me feel a whole lot better. I wasn't exactly happy, but I stopped gasping for breath, and such.

But how would I get there? It was fifty miles to Stratford. I could walk it in three days probably. But there was Pa's jolly boat. He'd moored it up on Baker's Cove, he said. It might still be there. The British might have found it, or somebody might have come along and just plain stole it. But it was worth a chance.

So I searched around in the cupboard for something to eat. There was a few apples and some cornbread. I wrapped them in Ma's kerchief and then I left the cabin and set off for Baker's Cove. Soon I came to the beach. The British ships was raising their sails and getting ready to head back to New York. Judging by the sun it was about halfway between sunrise and noon. I didn't want to go sailing down amongst the British ships, but I figured they'd be gone pretty soon. The tide was up and the air was fresh and salty. I walked along the beach for a ways. Sure enough, tied up under a willow tree, so that the branches hung down over it, was the jolly boat. It was sixteen foot long, and pretty wide, so's to have room inside for plenty of fish if you got a good catch. It was lateen rigged, which means the sail hung down from a yard about two thirds the way up the mast. Pa had painted a yellow band around it just below the gunnels for decoration.

I untied the boat, climbed in, and pushed off the bank with an oar. Then I hoisted the sail and swung out into the ocean. It was around thirty-five miles to New Haven, and maybe fifteen more to Newfield in Stratford, where Aunt Betsy lived with Captain Ivers. Ma had told me about the place lots of times. Captain Ivers had a wharf by the shore in the Newfield part of Stratford, and a warehouse, and a black brig. I figured I'd recognize it.

I could see the British fleet clear now. Their sails was full and they was moving down past the river into the Sound where the ocean was cut off by Long Island. The wind was from the southwest, so's I couldn't run straight down but had to tack back and forth, staying in close to shore as much as I could in case something went wrong.

I sailed all day that way, feeling lonely and sad, but determined to get there. When the sun was overhead, I pulled into a little creek to look for fresh water. I dipped the bread in the water to soften it, and ate it and the apples.

As I sat there eating, it came to me: What if Aunt Betsy wouldn't take me in? What if they didn't have no place for me? Or what if Captain Ivers, her master, didn't want no more niggers around?

I decided not to let myself think of that. I took a big drink of water out of the creek to store up, and set off again.

For a long time I could see the British fleet ahead of me, pushing toward New York. They was going faster than me, but it took them hours to pull away. Oh, I hated seeing them. Finally the ships dwindled down to sails, and then, by the middle of the afternoon, the sails was gone, too.

I sailed on. I went past New Haven, which looked even bigger than New London, with two long wharves sticking out into the water and behind them a great patchwork of roofs with three or four church steeples sticking up out of them. I couldn't see but one sloop in the harbor; I guess the rest had got sunk in the war.

I went on sailing, watching the sun set, and the light fade out in the sky, and by and by I came to the mouth of a big river opening out into the Sound. I figured it was the Housatonic. I'd heard Pa talk about it. I knew that Newfield wasn't much further along; and sure enough, in fifteen minutes, here came a wharf with a black brig tied up to it, and on shore a warehouse facing out to sea.

I headed the jolly boat in and beached it on the sand alongside the wharf, and climbed out. I was feeling mighty cramped from sitting in the jolly boat all day, but oh so glad I'd soon be with somebody. I had a good stretch, twisting and squirming with my arms over my head, and then I walked up the beach to the warehouse and found a little path there. Back across a field I could see lights. I walked along the path until I could make out a brown shingled house in the dark.

Then I stopped, and began to worry all over again. Suppose they didn't want me after all? Suppose Aunt Betsy didn't love Ma so much as Ma thought? Besides, she'd never met me and didn't know me from a goat. Suppose they didn't need no extra mouths to feed? But I was lonely and tired and I wanted to be with somebody as bad as could be. So I slipped around behind the house. There was a barn there. Somebody was moving around in it with a lantern. I crept up to the barn door and took a peek inside. There was a little black boy there in the lantern light, pitching hay into a stall where a cow was tied up. I figured he must be my cousin Dan.

I stepped into the barn. He sort of jumped around and looked at me. "You're Dan, ain't you?"

"Yes, sir," he said.

It kind of surprised me to be called sir. Nobody had ever called me that before. But he was only seven and I guess I looked like a grown-up to him. "I'm your cousin Willy from Groton," I said.

His eyes went wide. "Cousin Willy?"

"Where's your Ma?" I said.

"She's in the kitchen fixing supper for the Iverses, sir."

For the first time in a while I felt like smiling. "You don't have to call me sir," I said. "I ain't a boy. I'm a girl."

"Oh," he said. He looked kind of doubtful. "I'll tell Ma you're out here." He dropped the pitchfork and ran past me out of the barn and through the back door into the house. And in about five seconds Aunt Betsy came running out, wiping her hands on her skirt.

I went out towards her. For a moment we stood there in the dark, with only the light from the lantern making shadows on our faces, just looking at each other. Then she said, "Willy?"

"Yes, ma'am," I said. "It's me."

"I would have known, anyway," she said. "You're the spittin' image of your Ma." Then we came together and hugged. It felt mighty good to be hugged again.

She pulled back. "We heard about Fort Griswold. Did your Ma send you down here?"

"No, ma'am," I said. "I came by myself. The British took Ma down to New York."

She put her hands over her face. "Oh, no," she said. "I was scared it would be like that. We heard terrible stories, but we didn't know what to believe."

"Pa's dead," I said. "They killed him. I saw it. They stabbed him in the back and—" I started to choke and quit talking. Aunt Betsy put her arms around me again and held me like I was a baby. I wished I was a baby, too, and had somebody to look after me and didn't know about all the terrible things that had happened.

"What are you going to do now, Willy?"

I lifted up my head and looked at her face, all yellow in the lantern light. "I figured on staying with you," I said. "I'll work hard."

45

She looked sad and shook her head. "I don't know, Willy," she said. "I don't know what Captain Ivers'll say about that. I wouldn't want to trust him none."

Just then there came around the corner of the house a big black man wearing white army trousers and an old shirt. I knew it must be Uncle Jack.

"It's Willy, Jack," Aunt Betsy said. "Jordan got killed at Fort Griswold and the British took Lucy down to New York."

He didn't say nothing, but looked at me, and then he put his arms around me and gave me a big hug. "You poor child," he said. I was mighty glad I'd come there.

5

It was just luck that Uncle Jack Arabus was home when I got there. He was in the American army—the Fifth Company of the Third Regiment of the Connecticut Line, under Captain Bradley. There was seven or eight black men in the company, he said. There was lots of black men in George Washington's army. The rule was that they got themselves free if they would join up.

Uncle Jack had been staying way over in New York up along the Hudson near some place called Cold Spring. They'd furloughed the men home to get fresh clothes and new shoes. Uncle Jack, he'd already fought at Trenton and Stony Point, and some other places, too. They were fixing to fight again. Uncle Jack didn't know where, but he figured they might attack New

York to drive the British out. But there was no way of being sure.

They took me into the kitchen. There was a big brick fireplace, with a fire going, a rough wooden table where the Arabus family ate, big pans hanging up along the walls, and cupboards with pewter mugs and plates inside. It was nice to be with them, all warm and cozy, instead of all alone by myself on the water. Aunt Betsy fed me some corn bread and salt pork and I sat there and ate, kind of sniffling and putting out a little sob every once in a while. I told them the whole story: about seeing the British land and the battle and then Ma disappearing. And I'd just about got to where I was sailing off in the jolly boat, when a thin white woman, with a pointed nose, came into the kitchen. I figured she must be Captain Ivers's wife. She looked at me. "Who's this?" she snapped out.

"She's my sister's child," Aunt Betsy said. "Her name's Wilhelmina."

I got up and started to give a little curtsy, the way Ma had taught me, but in the middle of doing it I realized I couldn't because I didn't have no skirt on; so I bowed instead.

"Why's she dressed like a boy?" Mrs. Ivers sort of spit when she talked.

"She just came down from New London, ma'am," Uncle Jack said. "She was in the fighting. Her Pa got killed and her Ma taken off by the British."

Mrs. Ivers went on staring at me as if I was lower than dirt and she was afraid she'd soil herself just by looking at me. It made me mighty uneasy, that stare. "Well, she can't stay here," she said. "I'm not going to feed another lazy nigger. I've got enough of them as it is."

"She hasn't got anyplace to go, ma'am," Uncle Jack said, kind of quiet.

"I can't help that," Mrs. Ivers said. "I can't be responsible for any stray who happens up."

"Please, ma'am," Aunt Betsy said. "She ain't a stray. She's my sister's only child."

"Let your sister look after her, then," Mrs. Ivers said.

"But, ma'am," Aunt Betsy started to say, when Captain Ivers himself came into the kitchen. He was thin like Mrs. Ivers, but taller. His hair was silver, and his nose was pointed, too. "Someone left a lantern burning in the barn," he snarled. "Arabus, you go take care of that." Then he noticed me. "Whose nigger boy is this?" he said.

"She isn't a boy, she's a girl," Mrs. Ivers said.

"She's kin, sir," Uncle Jack said. "Her Pa was killed yesterday at Fort Griswold fighting the British." Then he went out the door.

Now it was Captain Ivers's turn to stare at me in that way his wife had. He stared for a while, thinking, his face dead still, like a frozen pond. Then he said, "Whose nigger are you?"

"Nobody's, sir." I said. "We're free niggers."

The captain thought about that for a minute with that frozen look. Then he said, "You sure you didn't run away when you had a chance during the fighting?"

"No, sir," I said. "Colonel Ledyard, he set us all free four years ago so Pa could join up with the army."

"It'll be easy enough to check that with Ledyard," he said.

"Colonel Ledyard, he's dead," I said. "Some British officer killed him with his own sword. I saw it."

He stared at me some more, thinking. It was amazing he could hold his face so still. Talking to him was like splashing eggs off ice; they didn't leave no mark. Finally he said, "How'd you get down here, anyway?"

"I came down in Pa's jolly boat, sir."

"By yourself?"

"Yes, sir."

"She can't stay here," Mrs. Ivers put in.

"Be quiet, Mother," Captain Ivers said. "Don't trouble yourself with making decisions." He looked up at the ceiling and rubbed his neck, which was the most expression he'd shown so far. Then he said, "The colonel left a widow, I suppose?"

"Mrs. Ledyard?"

"What sort of idiot are you?" he snapped. He snatched at my ear and gave it a twist. It hurt mighty good, but I knew better than to cry out. "Who did you think I was talking about?"

"She's alive, sir," I said. "Unless she got killed."

He let go of my ear. "She's from New London?"

"No, sir," I said. My ear smarted and I wanted to rub it, but I didn't dare. "The Ledyards are from Groton, across the river from New London."

"I know where Groton is," he said. "Don't advise me."

"No, sir," I said. Oh, he was making me mad and I felt like arguing back, but there wasn't nothing I could do about it.

Suddenly Mrs. Ivers got her courage up and said, "I don't want her in my house," which would have been all right by me.

"She's staying," Captain Ivers said. "Until I decide what to do with her." He gave Mrs. Ivers a look. She looked mighty cross, but she didn't dare go against him.

"Very well, Father," she said. "If she's staying, she's going to work for her supper, I promise you that." Captain Ivers didn't pay any attention to her, but went away. She turned to Aunt Betsy. "She can start by scrubbing the floors. And put her in a dress. This is a God-fearing home and I won't have anybody under my roof dressed unnatural." Then she stomped out of the kitchen.

We sat there quiet for a moment, Aunt Betsy and Dan and me. Then Aunt Betsy said, "I don't like it none, Willy. He's got something in mind for you."

I didn't have to ask what it was. Captain Ivers was trying to figure a way to put me back into slavery. I didn't know what he'd do with me once he'd done it—sell me off to the West Indies most likely. The trouble was, I didn't have no freedom papers. I knew I was free, but that didn't prove it. Pa had papers hid up in the cabin somewhere, but that wasn't no use to me now. And even if I had them, I couldn't read them, so I wouldn't know what they said. "What can I do?" I said.

Aunt Betsy shook her head. "I don't know what you can do, Willy. All I can say is, it's going to be mighty risky for you to stay around here."

I thought about the jolly boat, tied up at the wharf. "Maybe I could go down to New York and find Ma."

She shook her head again. "You couldn't hardly do that, Willy. The British have it. There's thousands of troops there. They set the town alight twice and half burned it down. There's hardly anything to eat, either, even for the British. You'd never find her, and the chances are you'd starve, too."

"I might find her, though."

"You'd never get through. There's skirmishing and such going on all around the city. If you asked too many questions, you might get hanged for a spy. We know about it. Your uncle Jack, he has a friend down there, Black Sam Fraunces. He owns about the biggest tavern in New York. The British let him go in and out of the city so's he can search out food for the tavern. A lot of the officers eat there. He came up to where your uncle Jack was stationed with General Washington and told Jack about it."

"Maybe Mr. Fraunces would help me find Ma," I said. "Maybe he'd know where she was."

"It's rough down there, Willy," Aunt Betsy said. "It ain't no place for a girl to be wandering around in."

I knew I shouldn't argue with her—she was a grown-up, and I was just a child. But there was this picture in my head of me coming along some street in New York and suddenly here comes Ma, and we run up and hug each other. Just thinking about it gave me a lovely feeling. I wanted to be with her so much I could hardly stand it.

Another reason for leaving there was that the whole Arabus family slept down in the Iverses' cellar on heaps of straw. It was a mean, damp place down there and bound to be cold in the winter. I wasn't used to it; I was used to having a cabin of our own, and a real straw mattress. I was worried I'd take sick living down in a cellar like that.

The next day Mrs. Ivers put me to work scrubbing floors. I hated it. If it had been Ma who made me scrub floors, I wouldn't have minded so much, because it would have been for a good reason; and if I was getting paid for it, it would have been all right, too. Being ordered around by Mrs. Ivers like I was a slave again made me mad, and it was all I could do to keep from shouting at her. But I knew if I did that she'd twist my ear and maybe beat me, too, so I made myself keep quiet.

Captain Ivers, he was down at his warehouse all morning. He came back at lunchtime and into the parlor where I was scrubbing. "Stand up," he said.

"Yes, sir," I said.

There wasn't no skirt for me so I was still wearing my milking britches. He looked me up and down like I was some kind of livestock for sale. Then he stared at me with that cold face. "Colonel Ledyard's dead, you say."

"Yes, sir," I said. "I seen it. They ran him right through side to side, and he dropped—"

"A simple 'Yes, sir' is enough." He stared at me some more, his mouth curved down tight. "And he promised your father his freedom."

"He didn't promise," I said. "He set us—"

He reached out and cuffed me on the side of the head. "A simple yes or no." He stared some more. "I suppose you have papers," he said.

"Oh, yes, sir," I said. I wanted to go on about it, but I didn't want to get hit no more.

"Where are they?"

"In our cabin, sir," I said.

He nodded, and then he turned and walked away. I dropped back down to the floor and started scrubbing, and I knew I'd just better get out of there as fast as ever I could. It seemed likely to me that Captain Ivers would take over Pa's jolly boat as soon as he could figure out a way to make a claim for it.

But Uncle Jack and Aunt Betsy were against me going down to New York. Uncle Jack had to go off back to camp, so I had to find a chance to talk to him quick. The first time I was with him alone I brought it up. "I figure I could make it in the jolly boat," I told him.

"It's too risky, Willy," he said. "You'd best forget

about it. We'll think of something else. Where would you stay in New York?"

"Aunt Betsy said you're friends with Black Sam Fraunces."

"Yes, but Sam, he's got a tavern to run. He ain't going to have time for no runaway. I want you to forget about it, Willy."

But I wasn't going to forget about it. I kept getting that picture in my head of going along a street and seeing Ma coming toward me. I was resolved to go: but even with Uncle Jack gone, I would still have to slip away from Aunt Betsy and the Iverses.

It was hard to make a run for it. Captain Ivers was down at the warehouse all day long, early morning until near dusk, where he could see anyone on the beach. And Mrs. Ivers, she hardly ever left the house. So two or three days went by and I got more and more worried—scared that he'd find a way to take the jolly, scared he'd find a way to sell me off.

Then, around the fourth day, Captain Ivers came up to the house toward suppertime. The sun was setting. Aunt Betsy was cooking stew over the fire in the kitchen. Dan was out in the barn feeding the cow, and Mrs. Ivers was in her bedroom reading her Bible. Then Captain Ivers came in the back door. "Where's Dan?" he said. "I want him to take a message for me."

I saw my chance. "He's in the barn, sir," I said. "I'll take it."

He gave me a suspicious look. He wasn't used to nobody offering to do anything, and he didn't trust it. But he said did I know where Dr. Beach's house was, and I said I did, which was a lie. So he went into the front room and wrote out a note, and then he folded it over and gave it to me, and told me to be quick about it.

There was an old coat hanging by the kitchen door that Aunt Betsy used when she was outside in the cold weather. I hated taking it from her, because she needed it, but I knew I'd like to freeze to death out there on the Sound without it. So I put it on.

"Hurry back so's you can help with supper," Aunt Betsy said.

"I will," I said. I wanted to hug her good-bye, but of course I couldn't do that. So instead I took a good look at her face, to memorize it so I could remember what she looked like. Then I went outside. The barn door was open and I could see Dan in there with the pitchfork, throwing hay in to the cow. I wanted to hug him, too, but I couldn't do that, either. So I just gave him a wave and he waved back, and I trotted down the path toward the beach, my heart beating fast.

In a couple of minutes I was on the beach. The jolly boat was still where I had left it. For a minute I stood there looking around. There was nobody in sight. The sun was just going down and a light night breeze was springing up. Captain Ivers's brig rocked in the waves lapping around the wharf. I'd have a fair wind for sailing.

I tossed Captain Ivers's note onto the beach and ground it down into the sand with my foot. Then I climbed into the jolly, hoisted the sail, and I was off.

The wind was coming out of the south and I could make pretty good time on a reach. I angled out until I was about a half mile from shore—far enough so's nobody on shore could tell who I was or where I'd come from. Then I pointed her west down the Sound toward New York. I reckoned I'd only been gone fifteen minutes. They'd begin to miss me pretty soon, but they wouldn't miss me yet.

I was mighty sorry to be alone and cold again. I began to miss Aunt Betsy and Dan almost as much as I missed Ma. But I missed her the most, and even if I was alone and cold, I was headed toward her.

The sun had got down now. The sky was all streaks of red and pink, mighty pretty, too. But the darkness was rising up behind me fast, the wind was chilly, and I knew it wasn't going to be no fun. There was lights here and there along the shore. I slid past a couple of little villages. It got darker, and behind me to the east a few stars was out. Pretty soon it'd be too dark to sail—there was too big a chance of hitting something in the water that'd punch a hole in the boat. I'd have to pull into an inlet and hide until morning came. And I was looking along the shore, through the dark, trying to spot a good place, when I heard oars creaking.

I stood up in the jolly with my hand on the tiller and looked around. The sound was coming from somewheres toward the shore ahead of me, off the starboard bow. I stared through the dark, and then I began to see the shape of sails, just gray patches in the starlight. They was coming out from shore and they was traveling mighty fast, with sails and oars going all at once. There was five or six boats, and they wasn't no little dories, either, but whaleboats thirty feet long. I swung into the wind and let the sail luff to stop me from running up to them. On they came, lickety-split. Now I could see the outlines of them against the sky. There was maybe thirty men in each of them, with eight or ten on a side at the oars. Right then I realized what it was: a big raiding party of Americans crossing the Sound to hit the British on Long Island.

Then I heard a low shout, and the next thing I knew the whaleboats had turned and was heading right toward me.

6

I CAME ABOUT TO make a run for it back up the Sound the way I'd come, but I didn't have no chance. The next thing I knew they was all around me, speaking in low voices. They shipped oars, grabbed hold of the sides of the jolly boat, hauled me out and dumped me on the bottom of one of the whaleboats.

I lay there on my back, staring up at the sky. I could see the top of the mast of the jolly boat slipping away out of sight and I knew I'd never see it again. The first thing I thought was that Pa would like to kill me when he found out; and then it hit me that he was dead himself and wouldn't never find out. Just then one of the men hunkered down beside me, his face so close to mine I could hear him breathe and see the whites of his eyes shine in the starlight.

"Where you coming from, boy?" he said in a low, scary voice.

I didn't want to tell them I was a runaway—there was no guessing what they'd do then. But I didn't have much of an idea where I was, so it was hard to make up a good lie. "I was trying to find my friends, sir, but I got lost in the dark."

"What friends? Where do they live?" still keeping his voice low.

I decided to come as close to the truth as I could. "Stratford, sir."

"You're a long way from Stratford, boy. What're you doing way down here?"

"Like I said, sir, I must have slid past it in the dark. I was just putting into shore to ask somebody."

"He's a spy," a low voice in the dark said. "The niggers are all for the British. Throw him in the water and be done with it."

"Honest, I ain't a spy," I said.

"Hold up a minute, Ned," the man hunkered beside me said. "What were you going down to Stratford for?"

I knew I'd better convince them I was on the American side. "My Pa, he got killed at Fort Griswold and my Ma got taken away by the British. I was going to Stratford to find my aunt."

Nobody said anything for a minute and I knew they was thinking if they should believe it. Finally the man beside me said in that low voice, "That's the truth?"

60

"I saw it happen, sir," I said. "They stabbed him in the back and he flung his arms out, just so, and died."

The man beside me turned his head away. "Were there any niggers killed at Griswold, Ned?"

"There was some. Two or three, I think."

"All right, son. What time did the British get up there?"

"It was just around noon, I reckon, sir," I said. "They busted down the door and came pouring in, and when Colonel Ledyard tried to surrender, they ran him through with his own sword."

Nobody said anything for a minute. Then the one called Ned said, "That sounds right to me. I heard about it."

The man next to me rose up. "All right, son. You just lie there. Don't be moving around and don't make any noise. We'll decide what to do with you when we get back."

It was a raiding party, all right. They'd land somewheres on Long Island, bust something up, capture some British officers if they could, and run back across the Sound. I was going to find myself in the middle of a fight again.

And, of course, the chances was they'd take me back to Connecticut after the fight. There was no way of telling what would happen then. Maybe they'd find out I'd run off from Captain Ivers and send me back to him. Or maybe one of them would take me for a slave himself. Or I didn't know what all else. And then how would I get down to New York to find Ma? I had to escape; somehow, while I was over on Long Island with the raiders, I had to escape.

But there wasn't anything I could do about that right then. So I just lay on my back staring up at the stars and trying not to think about Pa. Oh, the stars were bright and beautiful and there was a sliver of silver moon coming up in the east. When the whaleboat rocked down on that side the silver sliver would suddenly rise up, like a slice in the sky; and then the whaleboat would rock back and it would disappear again. By and by it got high enough so's it was in view all the time and I lay there watching it and feeling the whaleboat rock in the waves; and after a while I dozed off.

I woke up to the crunching of pebbly sand under the keel. I opened my eyes and stared at the sky again. In the starlight I could see the shapes of men shipping their oars and jumping out of the boat onto the beach, talking in whispers and moving as quiet as they could. I took a chance and sat up. We was in an inlet. There was high bushes along the edge of the beach and woods beyond. I could hear more crunching, and I knew they was pulling the boats up across the sand and tucking them in under the bushes to hide them as best they could.

Somebody grabbed me by the shoulder. "Out of there now, boy." I stood up and climbed over the side of the boat and some men grabbed it and pulled it up into the bushes. Then they began to disappear silently off into the darkness. I wondered if they was going to just leave me behind, but then I noticed about twenty men standing by the boats, which they'd left for guards.

What should I do? Could I try to slip away in the dark? Or break and run for it in hopes they wouldn't want to shoot at me for the noise, and I'd get lost in the dark. Once I escaped I knew I could find New York just by heading west; I'd know which direction that was as soon as the morning sun started to come up.

The men wasn't paying much attention to me. They'd sent four of themselves off to stand guard out in the woods. The rest of them sat on the gunnels of the whaleboats or on the beach and talked together low. Some of them lay down in the bottom of the whaleboats and went to sleep. I'd had a rest and didn't feel too sleepy, so I sat on the gunnels of a boat, feeling the cool night breeze blowing across my skin and hearing the slap-slap-slap of waves on the shore. I began to wonder what was going to happen to me and what the war was about, anyway.

Who was it good for? Not me, I figured. I'd lost my Pa, killed, and my Ma gone somewheres, I didn't know where. On top of it, it looked like I'd been turned back into a slave. Although when I came to think about it, when you was a woman you was half a slave, anyway. You had to get married, otherwise you couldn't hardly support yourself, and after that your husband, he was the boss and you had to do what he said. That was so even for white women: Mrs. Ivers couldn't go against Captain Ivers no more than Ma could go against Pa. And of course, if you was black, you was down at the bottom, anyway.

When I looked at it like that, it seemed that it was the white men who was going to come out of it on top, the way they always did. The black men, leastwise the ones who fought and got their freedom, would come out second best, and the women wouldn't be no better off than they always was. I mean, if Uncle Jack got his freedom by fighting for the Americans and bought free Aunt Betsy and Dan, Mrs. Ivers wouldn't have nobody to be boss over no more. Not that I was likely to feel sorry for her: she was too hard and cruel for that. But still, she didn't have much to gain out of the war.

Why was they fighting, then? Well, I guess it was like children growing up: after a while, they won't do what their folks tell them to do no more. The way it looked to me, the Americans—leastwise the white men—figured they was grown up and shouldn't have to do what the British told them; and the British figured the Americans wasn't grown up and ought to obey. That was what the war was about. But no matter who won, it wouldn't leave the slaves no better off, nor the women, neither. It was a funny thing to me how people wanted to be free. If you was scrubbing a floor for your own self in your own cabin, why, that was all right; it didn't hardly seem like work. But if you was scrubbing somebody else's floor, it was just awful. Maybe somebody else wouldn't feel that way, but I did.

But thinking about being free wasn't getting me free. If I went back to Connecticut with the raiders, the chances was good that I'd end up with the Iverses again. I had to get out of there someways.

I looked around. The men wasn't paying any attention to me. They was just lounging around talking amongst themselves. The moon was down now and they was just shapes in the dark. If I could creep off a ways down the beach, they wouldn't be able to see me, and then I could slip into the woods and disappear. But creeping off wasn't going to be so easy.

Then I had an idea. I got up off the gunnel and strolled across the beach to the water's edge, like I wasn't going anywhere in particular. A couple of them glanced at me, and then went on with their quiet talk. At the water I crouched down, like I was going to wash my hands. Then I fumbled around in the sand until I got hold of three or four small rocks. I collected them up in my hands and strolled back to the boat where I'd been sitting and squatted down beside it.

I was pretty well out of sight of the men, except for the top of my head. Quickly I flung one of the pebbles off into the woods. It smacked off a tree and rattled down through the brush. The men stopped talking and froze. "What's that?" one of them hissed.

I flung another stone. It rattled through the brush like the other one. The men was on their feet now, their muskets up, staring off into the woods. "Who's there?" one of them said in a gruff voice.

I flung another stone off into the woods and listened to it click-click through the trees. "Somebody's out there," one of the men said. "Let's spread out." They formed a line, about ten feet apart, and the next thing I knew they was pushing off into the woods. Crouching low, I began to slip off down the beach. When I'd gone fifty feet, I turned and looked back. All I could see was the dim shape of the boats. I stood up and ran down the beach, tripping and stumbling and banging my toes on rocks and driftwood; and then, when I was hot and panting and sweaty, I stopped running, ducked into the woods, and pushed on into them.

With my hands out to feel for trees, I moved along as quick as I could, bumping into things and catching my clothes on twigs and branches. And by and by the woods ended and I was standing at the edge of a field. I looked out across. It was lighter than it had been down at the beach. There was a patch of gray sky in the east. Dawn was coming. I didn't like going out into the open, but I didn't have no choice.

So I started across the field as fast as I could go, and in a bit I came to the fence at the other end. Over the other side of the fence there was a little dirt road. I jumped over the fence and started down the road toward the west, moving at a pretty good pace, and a half hour later I came to a bigger road. There was signs here, but being as I couldn't read, I didn't know what they said. So I kept on going as near to a westerly direction as I could, and after I'd gone a little farther I realized I'd got clear of the raiders. I was free. Oh, my, that felt good, even if I was out somewheres all by myself.

I walked all day to the west, and slept in a barn that night, and walked all the next day. I didn't know how far I had to go; I just kept going west knowing that sooner or later I'd bump into Manhattan Island, where New York was.

I went through three or four little villages. There wasn't much to them—just a few clapboard houses and a little store and tavern and not much else. There was a lot of British soldiers around, too, lounging in the streets or going in and out of the taverns. Once I passed a detachment of them sitting in a field smoking pipes. Nobody paid me no mind. I just sort of slouched on through the villages like somebody sent me on an errand and I wasn't in no hurry to get back. Nobody bothered me. Mostly, though, there wasn't any people, just farms and fields and sometimes woodlots.

Once I got a ride with an old darky who was driving a wagonload of potatoes. When he let me down, he gave me a half dozen potatoes. I took them into another piece of woods and borrowed a light from a pile of smoldering cornhusks and made a little fire and roasted them. I ate two, and saved the other four down in my shirt. Oh, they tasted mighty good, them hot roasted potatoes.

Finally, toward the end of the afternoon, I began to

smell the salty, fishy smell of ocean water. I kept on going down the road I was on and after a bit I could see blue water ahead. The road carried me right there.

I was on a low bluff, looking down into a bay in a river. Across the river, about a mile away, was a long island, stretching out in front of me. Most of it was low hills, with farms and woods. But dead across from me was New York. It was the biggest place I'd ever seen. There was hundreds of houses and a dozen church steeples as far as I could count, and a lot of great stone buildings, some of them five stories high. There was docks sticking out into the river, with every kind of ship tied up to them.

On my side of the river there wasn't so much to see—just marshy beach, a little dock, and a few small boats out on the river. And anchored in the bay was some extra big ships. I knew right away what they was—prison ships.

They was loaded down with American prisoners. We'd been hearing about them prison ships all through the war—how the men was crowded in so close they couldn't hardly sleep, and eating rotten bread and spoiled pork. The windows was tiny so's nobody could escape, and in the summer the men was like to boil to death down there. It was too bad they couldn't save any of that heat for the winter, because then they half froze. There was always sickness in them prison ships, a half dozen men dead every morning and carted away to be buried in the riverbanks and their families never knowing what happened to them.

Of course, it came to me right away that Ma might be on one of them. Maybe the British had captured her back at Groton and brought her down and slung her into a prison ship. There wasn't any way to know for sure. Oh, the idea of her being on a prison ship, all crowded in, no clean air to breathe and eating rotten bread, was terrible. It made me feel so bad for her.

Still, there was no telling if she was on a prison ship. Maybe she was and maybe she wasn't, and the only way I could find out was to go and see for myself.

7

IT WAS LATE AFTERNOON and the sun was behind New York. Across the river it slanted off the roofs and windows so's the whole city sparkled like fire; and it shone off the ripples in the river, too, like sparks. It was a mighty fine sight, all magical and exciting, and I wished it didn't belong to the British, but was ours again. It wasn't right, them owning it, when it had been the people here who'd made it in the first place.

And then I began to wonder: Why was I on the Americans' side, anyway? What had the Americans ever done for me, except keep me at the bottom of the pile? I took one of the potatoes out from under my shirt and began to eat, thinking. There was Captain Ivers trying to put me back in slavery again, and nobody teaching me how to read or do sums, so's I couldn't even tell what town I was in without asking. And knowing I would have to take orders so long as I lived. Maybe in heaven black folks gave orders to white folks and women gave orders to men.

On the other side of it, Colonel Ledyard had freed us. That was mainly so Pa could join the army and get himself killed. Of course, the colonel didn't have to free me and Ma; he did that just to be fair. And it wasn't the Americans but the British who'd taken Ma off and maybe slung her into a prison ship.

When I thought about it that way it didn't seem to me that there was much difference between the British and Americans; and it wouldn't matter which of them won. But the truth of it was, I *felt* like an American. I didn't know why I felt that way, but I did. Maybe it was because Pa swore he was an American. I don't know. But I felt like an American and I wanted the Americans to win, and it made me angry that the British should have that sparkling city and not us, who made it.

Was Ma in a prison ship? The only way to find out was to go down there and ask. I didn't want to do it. I was mighty scared of going near the British—there was no telling what they might do to me. But I didn't have no choice. I wanted to see Ma so bad I was willing to look anywheres for her.

Down at the bottom of the bluff a rowboat had been tied up at the little dock and some British soldiers under an officer were loading boxes on it. I figured it was supplies for one of the prison ships. There was a road leading down the bluff to the dock. I went on down it and up to the British officer who was lounging there, watching the soldiers load the boxes. "Sir," I said, "do you know if there's any black women on any of them ships?"

"Black women?" he said. The soldiers was curious and they stopped working to listen.

"I'm looking for my Ma, sir."

"Your Ma?" the officer said. "Well, we don't keep women on prison ships. We British aren't animals, you know."

But I wasn't sure if he was telling me the truth. "None at all, sir?"

"Are you deaf, boy?" he snapped. "Didn't you hear what I said?"

"Oh, yes, sir," I said. "I heard."

"When I say something, I don't expect to be questioned on it."

"Yes, sir," I said. There wasn't going to be any arguing with him, I could see that. "Well, thank you, sir," I said. I started to turn to go back up the road, when he grabbed me by the arm.

"Where are you from, boy?"

I sure didn't want to say I was from Connecticut, which was rebel country. I didn't want to say I'd got carried over on a raiding party, neither. But I didn't know the names of any of the towns on Long Island.

73

So I just sort of waved my hand behind me and said, "Back there, sir."

"Back there?" he said. "What kind of an answer is that?"

"It ain't much of a place, sir," I said. "You wouldn't never have heard of it."

"Let's try and see."

"It's called Long Point," I said, which was the name of a place back home in Connecticut.

"Long Point?" the officer shouted. "I never heard of it. Where is it?"

"Back there a ways," I said. My lies wasn't going very well and I knew it.

"Come, come," he shouted in that way he had. "It's on Long Island, isn't it? The north shore or the south shore?"

I gave that a quick think. "More in the middle," I said.

"A point? In the middle of the island? You're lying. You came out spying. Guard, take hold of this boy," he shouted. "I think we might give you a taste of prison for a few days to see if we can't get a better story out of you." He gestured to the soldiers. "Take him out with you when you go," he snapped. Then he started to walk off up the road. One of the soldiers grabbed me by the arm and started to pull me toward the rowboat. The potatoes under my shirt started to slip and I grabbed at them through my shirt.

"Wait, sir," I cried. "I ain't a boy, I'm a girl."

The officer whipped around and the soldier let go of

my arm. The officer peered at me, looking me over. Finally he said, "By George, you are a girl."

I blushed. "Yes, sir," I said.

He shook his head, looking mighty annoyed. "Get out of here," he shouted. "Get out of here before I put you in prison anyway." He turned and strode off up the road, and I turned and started to follow after. But I hadn't gone more than a couple of paces when I felt something clutch my arm. I spun around. It was one of the soldiers.

He stared into my face. "So you're a girl?" he said.

I looked up the road. The officer was pretty far away already, striding along at a strong clip. I looked back down at the other soldiers. They was standing at the end of the dock, watching. I didn't say anything.

The soldier pushed his face close to mine. "So you're really a girl."

"Charlie, better leave her alone," another soldier said. "You'll get in trouble."

"I'm just trying to find out if she's a girl," the one called Charlie said. He'd now got his face so close I could smell the sweat and rum and pipe tobacco.

"Please," I said.

Suddenly he grabbed for my shirt at the waist and started to pull it off over my head. I wrapped my arms around my chest so's he couldn't get it off. "Please," I cried. "That was a lie. I ain't a girl, I'm a boy."

He reached his big hand up and touched me on the chest. "The hell you ain't a girl," he said. He grabbed my arms to unwrap them from my chest.

The other soldiers gathered around. "You better leave her alone, Charlie," one of them said. "You'll get in trouble."

Charlie turned to the other soldiers. "I ain't going to get in trouble. I'm just going to take her shirt off to see if she's lying." Quick while he was turned away I got one hand free and reached under my shirt and whipped out one of the roasted potatoes. I held it up. "See?" I said. "I ain't a girl. Look."

Charlie let go of me and grabbed the potato out of my hand. He scowled and the other soldiers busted out laughing. "Charlie, you're a blame fool," one of them said.

Charlie gave me a scowl, and then he turned and flung the potato way off into the water. I skipped out of there as fast as I could, leaving all the soldiers laughing and hollering at Charlie.

8

I RAN ALONG FOR a mile or so, until I figured I was well
away from the soldiers, and then I stopped and caught
my breath. It was pretty clear that I'd better go on
being a boy for a while, and in general try to lie as low
as I could and not attract attention. I'd got this far,
and I didn't want to mess it up.

But what was I to do next? The best thing would be
to get on across to New York and see what information
I could pick up there. The officer had said that there
wasn't no women on the prison ships. That might be
right and it might not; but the best thing would be to
get over to New York and see what people was saying.

How was I to get across? I didn't know. There must
be a ferry so I decided I'd go find it and see if maybe I

could work my way over or something. So I took up walking again, and by and by I came to a little village called Brooklyn. Leastwise, I found out later it was called Brooklyn. There was a fair number of houses and some taverns, and down at the end of the main street there was a ferry tied up at the dock. But it was coming on night and I reckoned there wouldn't be no ferries going over to New York until morning. So I slipped out behind one of the taverns and found a barn where they stabled horses. I borrowed a light from a lantern and made a little fire to heat my last two potatoes. It took a good long time for them to get hot, and after I ate, I was ready to sleep. I went up into the loft, and slept in the hay. I woke up at dawn and slid out of there before anybody could see me. I started on down the main street toward the ferry, and I'd only got a little ways when along came a wagon loaded with cordwood driven by a black boy. He was about my age, and mighty tall and skinny, so's he looked more like a length of rope than any human being.

I shouted up to him. "How much is the ferry?"

"Tuppence," he said. "I'm going down. Hop up and I'll give you a ride."

I climbed up. "Well, I ain't got tuppence," I said. "The fact is, I ain't got nothing at all. I didn't even have no breakfast."

He gave me a look and right away I knew he was suspicious of me. Most darkies, they wouldn't turn you in if they thought you was a runaway; most of them would help you if they could. But some would turn you in, and it was best to be cautious.

"How'd you reckon to get across if you didn't have no money?" he said.

"Well," I said. "I *did* have some money, but somebody stole it."

"How'd that come about?" he asked.

"I fell asleep along the road and somebody nipped it out of my pocket."

He had a way of twisting around and wrapping and unwrapping himself when he talked. He gave me another look. "Where'd you say you was from?"

"New York," I said.

He was still mighty suspicious. "Who's your master?"

That was a hard one. I didn't know nobody in New York at all, and I started to say I belonged to Mr. Brown, because there was bound to be somebody named Brown in New York, when I remembered Uncle Jack's friend, Black Sam Fraunces. "Mr. Fraunces," I said.

"Mr. Sam Fraunces?" He bent and twisted away from me and back again.

"That's him," I said.

He kind of scratched his forehead and looked at me some more. "I heard that Fraunces don't keep slaves."

"Oh, well, that's true," I said. "I ain't exactly his slave. I just work there."

He shook his head. "Well, you're about the worst liar I ever seen. I work for Mr. Sam Fraunces. That's where I'm going with this load of wood. You ain't never been within miles of the place."

It made me blush to be caught in a lie. But how was I to know he worked for Sam Fraunces? I put my hand on the edge of the wagon, getting ready to jump and run for it. "I ain't no runaway," I said. "I'm a free nigger."

"I don't believe that neither," he said, twisting away from me. "But I ain't going to tell on you. Where are you really from?"

I still didn't know whether to trust him or not. He sounded like he was safe enough, but there wasn't no point in taking a chance on it. For one thing, being as he was from New York, he might be a loyalist on the side of the British. It sure wouldn't do to tell him about Pa fighting at Fort Griswold. So I said, "I come from New London. My Ma got carried off by the British to New York, and I'm going down to look for her."

He gave me one of his twisty looks. "Where's your Pa?"

"He's dead." I didn't say how.

"New London is a mighty long ways from here," he said.

"I know that for sure," I said. "I came down as far as—well, I don't know where—in my jolly boat and some raiders caught me and carried me across to Long Island."

80

He unwrapped himself and laughed and slapped himself on the chest. "Well, you are the worst liar I ever heard in all my born days. Some raiders caught you, did they? Now I don't blame you for lying, if I was a runaway, I'd lie myself. But I can tell you ain't had much practice in lying, for you don't know anything about it."

He was making me feel mighty argumentative, but I could see there wasn't no use in telling the truth. So I said, "All right, if you're so blamed good about telling lies, make up a story for me."

He shook his head sort of solemn. "Now, the first thing about a lie is, it's got to be ordinary. You don't want to tell people you got caught by no raiders. You tell them that you came across with a load of hogs. There's nothing more ordinary than hogs. Besides, going with hogs lowers you some. That's another thing about lying. You always want to lower yourself. Don't tell people your money was stolen. You tell them that you got drunk and went to sleep in a ditch and when you woke up your money was gone. People will always believe anything like that."

"That's not so ordinary," I said.

"Around New York it's more ordinary than you think, especially with all them soldiers around and refugees and loyalists flooding in to be under the British, and nothing for none of them to do but get drunk and fall down and lose such money as they have. Besides, if it lowers you enough, it don't have to

81

be ordinary, people will believe it, anyway. Just so your lie lowers you, that's the main thing." He twisted around to look at me again. "Now tell me where you're really from."

There wasn't no hope in getting him to believe the truth. Still, I wasn't going to tell nobody I was a slave. "Well, if you really want to know, my Pa, he beats me most every time I turn around and finally I couldn't stand it no more so I ran off."

"Well, that's ordinary enough," he said. "Where'd you live at?"

I still didn't know the names of any places on Long Island, but he was from New York and didn't figure to know much about Long Island, either, so I said, "Long Point." This time I had enough sense not to put it in the middle of dry land. "Up on the Sound."

"What's your Pa do back there?"

I looked down at my lap, like I was ashamed of myself. "We was pig scrapers for a tanner."

He twisted away from me to watch the horse, looking satisfied. "Well, that's more believable," he said.

We had got down to the end of the main street, about a hundred yards from the ferry. It was a flat barge with an oar out each side, and a small sail, in case the wind was right. A couple of wagons was rolling onto it. "Well, I got to get down and figure out some way of earning tuppence."

He twisted around to look at me. "Look, if you get down in the middle of the wood, nobody'll see you and I'll carry you across. So long as you don't sneeze or do something foolish."

"That's mighty kind of you," I said.

He put out his hand. "My name's Horace," he said.

"Mine's Willy." We shook hands, and then I kind of hollowed out a little hole in the middle of the cord-wood and crept down there, and sat listening while the wagon creaked onto the flatboat. Then I heard the chain rattle as the ferry cut loose from the dock; and then oars creaking and little waves slapping on the hull; and then after a little while the chains rattling again, and the wagon creaked off the ferry and I was in New York at last.

We rode along a little ways, until we turned a corner. Then Horace told me to come out, and I climbed out and sat up on the seat beside him again, and we went along to Black Sam Fraunces' tavern.

It was a big building, bigger than anything in New London for sure. It was brick, four stories high, and four or five chimneys sticking out of the roof. There was big windows everywhere and a fancy door with windows over it, too. Horace read the sign out front. It said THE QUEEN'S HEAD, which was to suit the British while they was occupying New York.

We swung around back. There was a barn here for the horses and some sheds and a well, and such. I was beginning to feel nervous, and wondered what to do. What I ought to do, I knew, was get introduced to Mr.

Fraunces, and ask him about Ma. He was a big man in New York and would know how to find out if there was a black woman captured by the British somewhere. Besides, Uncle Jack knew him—leastwise he said he did—and Mr. Fraunces was likely to help me on account of that.

But it was pretty bold for somebody low as me to go marching up to somebody as high up as Mr. Fraunces and ask for help. Most probably he'd tell me he never heard of Jack Arabus, go away and stop bothering me. But even so, I knew I had to try it and it made me scared to think about it.

I helped Horace unload the cordwood and stack it alongside one of the sheds. Then he said, "You still ain't had nothing to eat."

"I'm pretty hungry," I said.

"Well, all right," he said. "You come on into the kitchen and I'll get you something."

"Will Mr. Fraunces mind?" I said.

"Mind? Mr. Fraunces? Why, I don't have to ask Mr. Fraunces about nothing like that. We're this close. He always says, 'Horace, you just go ahead and do what you think best.' He trusts me that much."

Well, I wondered about it: the story didn't seem to lower Horace none. But I didn't say anything.

We went into the kitchen. It was a big room, with a huge fireplace at one end and big pots hanging there steaming away. A couple of cooks was slicing apples at a big table. There was barrels of sugar and flour and molasses and such around, too, but I noticed they was pretty empty. "It was different before the war," Horace said. "Then we'd have a whole side of beef on a spit over the fire and apple pies and puddings and spice cakes and everything. But food's scarce now."

He grabbed up a couple of wooden plates from off a shelf and went down to the fireplace where the stew pots was, with me following along, getting hungrier by the minute from the smells. I hadn't had a proper meal for nearly four days. Just staring down at that stew bubbling away made me swallow hard. Horace grabbed up a ladle that was hooked over the edge of one of the stew pots.

Just then one of the cooks jumped over to us and snatched the ladle out of his hand. "Here, you boy, what do you think you're doing?"

"Hey," Horace shouted. "Mr. Fraunces says I was to help myself when I wanted."

Then a voice from behind us said, "Mr. Fraunces says you're to do what, Horace?"

We spun around. Standing at the door was a tall black man dressed in a blue suit with a silver buckle at his belt and ruffles on his chest. I knew right away it must be Mr. Fraunces, and my heart jumped.

I looked at Horace and back at Mr. Fraunces and then at Horace again.

Horace was wrapping his long self up and unwrapping himself a mile a minute. "Well, sir—well—I— sir," he said, and stopped there.

Mr. Fraunces looked at me. "Who's this?" he asked.

"He helped me unload the wood," Horace said. "He's hungry."

"I see," Mr. Fraunces said. "But we can't be feeding the entire populace, Horace. Food's scarce."

I was feeling mighty nervous, like I'd done something wrong, and I didn't know whether I ought to speak up about Uncle Jack or just scoot on out of there. I knew I shouldn't ought to miss my chance, but I was scared.

Mr. Fraunces didn't give me no time to think about it, for he walked over, took a look at me, and said, "When was the last time you had a meal, son?"

"I ain't had nothing much but a couple of roast potatoes the past two days."

"I see," he said. "Where are you from?"

It was now or never. "Sir, my uncle says he knows you. He's a soldier with General Washington. His name is Jack Arabus."

"Jack Arabus?" he said. "Why, I know Jack. Where is he now?"

"In camp. Up on the Hudson Highlands somewhere."

"And you're his nephew?"

It still took me by surprise when people called me a nephew instead of a niece, and I knew I'd better get used to it. "Yes, sir," I said.

I didn't know what to tell him. Was he on the American side or the British? Here he was running a tavern right in the middle of New York, which was owned by the British. On the other side of it, Uncle Jack would sure have told me if he was for the British. Unless maybe he'd changed over to the British side and Uncle Jack didn't know. A lot of people did that during the war—changed sides.

I decided to be cautious. So I said, "Well, I been staying with Uncle Jack up at Newfield in Stratford. My Ma, she was taken off by the British. Well, maybe she ran off with them, but I don't know. I figure she's down here in New York somewheres and I came down to find her."

"Your Ma went off with the British? How did that happen?"

I was getting into it more than I wanted, and I began to sweat a little. I figured I'd better be careful about telling lies: Mr. Fraunces was likely to be smarter about it than Horace. "We had some skirmishing up around where I'm from and I went and hid out and when I came back she was gone, and they said she went off with the British."

"Where was that?"

"Groton," I said.

He nodded his head. "That was a very sad business up there," he said.

"Yes, sir," I said. "I know it was. I saw some of it."

"I suppose you did," he said. He didn't say nothing for a moment. Then he said, "What's your name?"

"Willy." Then I said, "Willy Freeman," so's he knows I wasn't no slave.

"Horace, give Willy something to eat. Then send him around to my office."

Well, I felt like crying. For four days I'd been pushed around and chased, and swore at and shot at, too; and slept in boats and barns; and nothing to eat but potatoes and apples, and all of a sudden here I was in the fanciest tavern in New York, about to be fed on good hot stew. I could feel the tears come stinging up behind my eyeballs, and I had to rub my eyes, pretending I'd got some smoke in them.

So we sat down at a little table there in the kitchen and fed up on stew. Horace, he ate as much as I did, too, which was hard to believe. Him being so skinny and all, you wouldn't have thought he'd have enough stomach for it. I felt a lot better, just sitting there feeling warm and comfortable full for a change; then tiredness crept over me and I put my face down on the table and fell sound asleep.

By and by Horace woke me up. At first I didn't know where I was, and then I remembered, and sat there rubbing my eyes. "Mr. Fraunces wants to see you," Horace said. He led me out of the kitchen and down a back corridor to the end. There was a door there. He knocked on it and Mr. Fraunces said to come in and I did.

"Shut the door," he said.

It was a small room but pretty fancy, with a carpet on the floor and a polished desk, and a safe and bookshelves with glass doors on them and pewter sconces on the walls. There was a window that looked out on the barn and sheds in the back so's Mr. Fraunces could keep an eye on things. I could see Horace come out there and start hauling water out of the well.

Mr. Fraunces sat behind his polished desk, with his hands behind his head, looking at me. He didn't say nothing for a minute. Then he said, "Your Ma—she's Jack's sister?"

"No, sir," I said. "She's my aunt Betsy's sister."

"Ah," he said. "Jack's sister-in-law." Now that I got a good look at him in the light I began to notice something curious about him. His skin was dark, all right, but he didn't exactly look like a nigger. It was hard to tell: it seemed more like he must be part something else, too—Spanish or Portuguese, or Indian, maybe. But, like I say, it was hard to tell.

"You know, Willy," he said, "a lot of black people favor the British. They believe that the British will free them if they fight for them. Did you think you'd be better off with the British here in New York?"

Seeing as he'd asked me point blank, I was stuck. There wasn't no way out of it. I remembered what Horace said about lying—to make it ordinary, and lower myself. But I didn't know what kind of lie to tell and I decided I might as well tell the truth. "Sir, my Pa got killed by the British at Fort Griswold. I saw it myself. They stabbed him with their bayonets, and he flung his arms back like so—" I started to cry again and couldn't finish and stood there sobbing away like a fool. He didn't say anything and finally I got ahold of myself and stopped crying and wiped my face off with my sleeve.

"What was a young boy like you doing up there?"

"I ain't even a boy, sir," I blurted out. "I'm a girl."

He gave a kind of a jump. "A girl?"

"Yes, sir."

He stared into my face. "Why, I suppose you are," he said. "How on earth did you land in that battle?"

So I told him the whole story, about the British coming and me going to the fort to bring the horse back and the fighting and going down to Stratford and the rest of it. He just sat there listening. When I got done he didn't say anything for a minute, but thought about it all. Then he said, "Well, I guess you've had enough trouble for a while, Willy. We'll manage to put you up for a bit, until you can get settled."

"Thank you, sir," I said. "I'll work hard, I promise."

"I'm sure you will," he said.

"The main thing is, I got to find Ma." Once more I got the image of her coming along the street and us seeing each other and hugging.

He shook his head. "You don't even know she's in New York."

It was true. I looked at him, feeling discouraged. I guess it showed on my face, for he said, "Well, there are a couple of places you could try. And, Willy," he said, "I think it best that you stay a boy for a while."

9

I WAS TO STAY OUT in the barn with Horace. He said it
wasn't bad. There was horse blankets around that you
could roll up in, and the horses kept the place pretty
warm, even in the worst weather. There was cows in
the barn, too, and chickens and ducks. I was to help
out with the livestock and cleaning, and anything else
there was to do. I'd get my room and board and
maybe a few pennies, too, Mr. Fraunces said, if I did
my work well. I wasn't a slave, he said; I was free and
ought to get wages for my services, even if it wasn't
very much. I knew I wasn't expected to stay forever,
but Mr. Fraunces didn't seem in no rush to push me
off.

So I moved in. It worried me some, being up in the
barn loft with Horace. How was I to keep him from

finding out I was a girl, unless I slept in my clothes? And then, my shirt might slip up or something. It wasn't going to be easy.

Another thing I was worried about was getting a letter off to Aunt Betsy to tell her I was safe. Pa, he could write and cipher some, too, and was always intending to teach me, but never got to it. Horace claimed Mr. Fraunces had sent him to school and he could write. I figured I could get him to write me a letter.

So I settled in. I made up a story to tell folks, that I came from Long Island, my Pa beat me all the time and finally he died of the pox and I ran off to New York so's I wouldn't be put into slavery. I just had to be careful when I washed, or changed my clothes, that nobody was around. Horace was the main problem. He'd come up into the hayloft to go to sleep and strip off his clothes just as casual, and I'd have to fuss with my blankets so as not to see him naked. But he never noticed nothing. He wasn't much of a noticer.

I'd found out from Mr. Fraunces all the places that my Ma might be. He said he didn't think there was much chance she was on a prison ship, or one of the other prisons they had around the city. He said she *might* be there, but it wasn't likely. The British didn't usually put women into prison with men.

If she'd really come to New York, he reckoned, the most likely place for her to be was Canvas Town, over to the west side of the city. Just around the time the British were driving the Americans out of New York, there'd been a terrible fire. Nobody knew how it started. The British blamed the Americans and the Americans blamed the British. Mr. Fraunces, he figured it got started by accident. The wind caught it wrong, and it spread all around and five hundred houses burned down before they could stop it. That made houses in mighty short supply. Of course when the British came in, a lot of rebels ran off, leaving their houses empty. But in came the British troops and a lot of loyalists from other states, to be under British protection. A lot of plain drunkards, prostitutes, and roustabouts came in, too. There wasn't near enough housing for everybody, and people went over to the burned-out area and stretched canvas sailcloth over the chimneys and walls that was left standing to make places to live in.

There was a lot of black folk living in Canvas Town, Mr. Fraunces said. Black workmen made no more than a shilling and a half a day, where the whites made four shillings, and a lot more if they were blacksmiths or sawyers or skilled in some ways. So the blacks, being poorer, was likely to live in Canvas Town. And maybe my Ma was there, too. I resolved to go there as soon as I could, but the tavern was a mighty busy place.

Along about this time we got the news that Cornwallis had surrendered his army to General Washington at Yorktown. When that happened, everybody knew that the British wouldn't fight much more. Still, we knew that it would be a while before they actually

settled the thing and declared peace. In the meantime
the British didn't have nothing to do but sit around,
and they was always at the tavern drinking punch and
playing cards, and making us jump. So for a while I
wasn't able to get away to go look for my Ma.

But then there came a day when there was to be a
big ball at some other tavern. It would be pretty quiet
for us, and Mr. Fraunces said Horace and I could have
some time off in the afternoon, if we got our work
done. It was my chance to go to Canvas Town.

I was pretty uneasy about going over alone. It was
rough there, with drunkards and thieves and such. I
told Horace what I was planning to do, figuring he'd
be curious, and wouldn't want to be left out of an
adventure. He said he'd go, and as soon as we got
finished bringing in the wood and water, we left.

It was the middle of October. The sky was overcast
with clouds, and looked like rain, but it wasn't too
cold. We walked up Broad Street and over Beaver
Street. It was the first chance I'd had to get a look at
New York. I'd ridden into it under a pile of wood and
hadn't gone anywhere since. A lot of buildings were
three and four and even five stories high, mostly wood
or stone, but there was new brick ones mixed in, too.
The streets was narrow and dirty and there was hogs
and dogs and even cows running loose in them. It was
crowded—people going along carrying things, and
carts and wagons in the streets and drovers coming
along with cattle or sheep.

Horace, he knew all about everything we saw as we walked along. That man was old such-and-such; he was a known smuggler and had killed six men. That apothecary shop was no ordinary apothecary shop; it was a place where they ground up dead bodies and such to make potions that you could slip into somebody's drink and make them go crazy and die in a frenzy. He just rambled on like that the whole way along, and by and by we came to Canvas Town.

It was a pretty mean-looking place, and scary, too. It was a forest of chimneys, with here and there part of a brick or stone wall standing. There wasn't no wood in sight at all. There was an awful shortage of firewood in New York, because of the war, and the people who lived in Canvas Town had burned up any wood left over from the fire long before. Everywhere you looked you could see sailcloth stretched from walls and chimneys to make little shelters. The streets was just a field of mud. You could hardly push a cart through, it was so deep and thick. Over the whole place was a smell of charcoal and old garbage and rotten stuff. You wouldn't think anybody could stand living in a place like that, but they did. There was people everywhere, skirting around through the mud or standing around talking. I figured they was outside because it was gloomy under those tents, and they wouldn't go inside unless they had to. It was better to stay outside, even on a gloomy day like that one. They were smoking pipes, a lot of them, even the women, and some of them were drinking from bottles of rum.

We stood there at the edge of the place, staring around. Some people looked at us, but they didn't pay us no mind. We were just a couple of black boys, and wasn't worth more than a glance.

"I ain't much interested in walking around in all that mud," Horace said. "There's no telling what you might step on—a dead body, probably."

"Horace," I said, "there ain't so many dead bodies in all the world as you've provided today."

"Willy, you don't know nothing about it. This here place is filled with dead bodies. When they die, they just push them down into the mud. You could walk on dead bodies from one side of Canvas Town to the other."

Well, I didn't believe it. Still, hearing him talk like that scared me some. But if my Ma was there, I wanted to find her. "I'm going in, anyway," I said. I started along the street, trying to keep close to the burned-out walls, where there'd been less traffic and it wasn't so muddy. I figured Horace would follow me: he wouldn't want to be left out of anything. After a bit I looked over my shoulder, and sure enough, he was coming along after me, and in a minute he caught up.

We went on a ways, passing people perched up on broken walls, or picking their way through the mud the way we was doing. Finally I came to a big black man sitting on a broken brick wall, smoking a pipe and admiring the view. He had a scar on his chin, his nose was busted over and half his teeth was missing. He looked mighty rough.

Stretched back from the wall was one of them tent shelters. Right next to where his feet dangled down there was a hole in the wall where there'd been a window once, to make a kind of door for the tent.

"'Scuse me sir," I said. "I'm looking for a pretty nigger woman. She's about thirty—"

He began to chuckle without taking the pipe out of his mouth, puffing and blowing smoke with his chuckles, until some of it got sucked down the wrong way and choked him. He took the pipe out of his mouth, coughing and choking, and waved it at us. "Damn you," he shouted between coughs. Then he twisted down and shouted into the window hole, "Rum."

In a moment the head and shoulders of a woman popped out through the hole. She handed out a flask. The man snatched it away and took a long drink, which didn't seem to do him any good, for it made him choke some more.

The woman stayed there in the window, looking at us. She was pretty young—younger than Ma, I reckoned—but her face was bruised and swollen and her hair didn't look like it had been combed for days. Her dress hadn't been washed for a long time, neither, for it was splotched with food and mud. "What're you two doing here?" she said.

"I'm looking for my Ma," I said.

The man on the wall stopped choking. "She ain't

97

here," he said. "There ain't no mothers in Canvas Town." He put the stopper back in the flask and handed it to the woman. "Don't touch it, you slut," he said.

She took the bottle, turned away a little so's he couldn't see her, and licked the bottle around the top where a little rum had dribbled down. Then she said, "Don't pay him no mind. Who's your Ma?"

The man took the pipe out of his mouth and glared at us, looking mighty fierce. "I said there wasn't no mothers in Canvas Town." He put the pipe back in and sucked at it to make it go.

The woman lowered her voice. She had a bad fever, I could tell that. "Who is she?"

"Lucy Freeman is her name," I said. "She's from Groton, Connecticut. She's pretty, too, kind of chocolate-colored skin."

"She won't be pretty if she's down here long," she said.

The man sucked hard on his pipe, making it squeak. No smoke came out. "Damn," he said. He twisted down toward the woman again. "Give me a coal for my pipe."

"Fire's out," she said.

"You slut," he shouted. "Why's the fire out?"

"No wood," she said.

He slid off the wall into the muddy road and tromped off, looking for a coal to light his pipe with. The minute he had his back to us, the woman leaned farther out of the hole and grabbed my arm. "Now

98

listen," she said. "I seen your Ma," she said, kind of excited. "She was around just the other day. I'm sure it was her. A pretty woman from Connecticut."

"That's right," I said. I wasn't sure I ought to believe her, but I couldn't help feeling excited.

"Now you listen," she said, clenching my arm tight and staring at me. "You come back tonight, and bring me a few coppers for my medicine. I'll scout around and see what I can find. You understand?" She gave my arm a squeeze. "A few coppers for my medicine, understand?" She looked down the road. "He's coming back," she whispered. "But he won't be here tonight, he'll be off looking for rum. So you come back after dark. And bring me a few coppers."

"Yes," I said.

She let go of my arm. "Now run, before he catches you."

We turned and trotted back through the mud the way we'd come. We were both mighty anxious to get out of there, and we hustled straight on back to Mr. Fraunces' tavern.

I didn't know what to believe. At suppertime Horace and me helped the cook in the kitchen serve out the food. We wasn't allowed to go out into the dining room. They had waiters, dressed up in red jackets, that carried the food back and forth. But I'd snuck out there a few times when there wasn't nobody around. I tell you, it was a mighty fine room. There was glass chandeliers filled with candles hanging down from the ceilings, polished walnut wall panels with designs carved into them, and tables where the officers and rich folk sat to eat. Horace, he said that someday he was going to be a waiter, too, and wear one of them red jackets. Mr. Fraunces had promised, he said. But I knew I'd never be one, unless I wanted to stay dressed up like a boy the rest of my life. Women wasn't allowed to be waiters.

So we worked in the kitchen and I thought about the woman in Canvas Town, and between times I went over it with Horace. "Do you think she's lying, Horace?"

"Well, that's hard to say," he said. "Maybe she was, and then again maybe she wasn't."

"That ain't no help, Horace," I said.

"Well, I *know* it *ain't*," he said. "That's the idea of it. You shouldn't be too helpful to people—you should let them think things out for themselves. Otherwise you're to blame if it don't work out in the end. Now, you take somebody like me, Willy, who's spent all of his life in New York and knows how things is done and where the pitfalls lie, why, I'd know just how to decide a thing like that. But you ain't had the experience. So my advice to you is to think it through real careful, and then decide."

That wasn't no more use than the other, but I knew better than to say so, for if I did, he'd carry on in the same way until my head ached. So I did what he said. I thought it through careful, and in the end I decided I didn't have no choice—I had to go back down there and find out. For if that woman really did know where Ma was, it'd be just terrible to miss her.

So after we'd finished up with the suppers and got the dishes cleaned and the kitchen scrubbed out, we helped ourselves to some stew and sat there at the little table in the kitchen, talking in low voices. "I'm determined to go, Horace."

He frowned down into his stew, and thought about it awhile, and then he said, "Well now, Willy, I just knew that was the decision you'd come up with. I knew it. I knew you'd work it through and come out the wrong way. I knew it all along and I let you go ahead and do it, because I knew there ain't no way you can talk sense into nobody until they've worked their way through it theirself. Then you can come in and set them straight."

He didn't fool me none. He wished now that he'd discouraged me from going down there right off, because it was coming to him that if I went he'd have to go along with me and lend the coppers, besides. He didn't want to go down there at night any more than I did—less, because he didn't have nothing to gain out of it, and a good deal to lose. So I said, "What's wrong with going down there?"

He frowned over his stew, folded himself up, and unfolded himself again. Then he said, "There's a lot of things wrong with it. There's a good chance we might get killed. That's what's wrong with it."

"Oh, nobody's going to bother with a couple of nigger boys. There wouldn't be no point in it—we ain't got anything worth stealing."

"You don't know them people down there like I do. They'd kill you just to see the blood flow."

It kind of made me shiver to hear that, because I knew it was partly true. I figured there was bound to be some of them down there that would kill for nothing, especially when they was drunk—oh, maybe not mean to kill you, but push you around just to scare you and push you too hard. But I was determined to go, and I wanted him to go with me, because I was mighty frightened about going down there alone. So I said, "You're just scared of it, Horace."

He unfolded himself so's he could look me in the eye. "You bet I'm scared," he said. "And if you had any sense, you'd be scared, too."

"Well, I'm going," I said. "And you're going, too."

"Maybe we ought to think it over for a few days."

"No," I said. "We maybe would never find that woman again. We're going tonight."

He folded himself back over his stew, looking pretty gloomy. "I reckon you'll want to borrow some coppers, Willy."

"That's mighty good of you to think of it, Horace," I said. "I wouldn't have thought of it myself."

He got the sourest look on his face and I nearly busted out laughing. But I knew better than to do that, for fear of getting him mad at me, so I didn't say nothing. He went off to the hayloft to get some coppers out of a handkerchief he'd got them tied up in and hid down in the hay, and I took from the kitchen a couple of candle ends and a little lantern with dozens of tiny holes poked through the tin, and we set off.

It was still overcast, and there wasn't no moon at all, nor no stars, either. A little fog was drifting in from the river, like floating spirits. There was oil lights along the streets every fifty feet and the thin fog made them shine like small white balls. There was pigs sleeping here and there in the streets, and dogs that stood in cellarways and barked at us, and a few people hurrying along silent with their cloaks pulled up over their faces against the fog and looking around for fear of robbers. And about every two minutes I'd have a feeling for turning around and going back. But I'd made Horace go out with me, and I didn't dare back down.

Horace kept twisting himself around on the lookout for robbers, until I thought he would wind himself up like a spring. He wasn't watching the ground and he stumbled and cursed, which was a thing he wouldn't have done if he'd known I was a girl. Then he'd whisper that we was a pair of fools and ought to be put in the lunatic house for it. And I would say there wasn't nothing lunatic about looking for your mother, and we'd go on.

Finally we came to where Canvas Town began. Here and there they'd put up pitch pine torches that snapped and flickered amongst the forest of chimneys, making the shadows of them waver on the walls. The fog drifted in wisps among them, pale white. Oh, it was terrifying. My heart was beating real fast and I wondered if Horace was right, that we hadn't ought to have come.

But there wasn't no way to turn back, so I started along the muddy street toward the place where the sick woman lived, holding the little lantern so I could see the broken walls as I went. Horace came along close behind me. Lights shone through the canvas of some of the tents, so's we knew they'd got fires going inside, or at least candles. There was voices coming out of them, too, laughing or shouting or arguing. There wasn't many people in the muddy streets—just two or three that jumped out of the dark at us and went on by.

All the tents looked the same and it was hard to tell which one was the sick woman's. A couple of times we came to places where there was a hole in the wall, and we'd think it was hers; but when we held the lantern inside, they was empty, just some straw in there and a couple of empty bottles glistening in the light.

Finally we hit one that seemed like it must be it. "I think this is the one," I said.

"I surely hope so," Horace said.

I bent down and reached in with the lantern. I could see somebody in there, sleeping, but pretty indistinct. "I think it's her," I said. "I'm going in. Hold the lantern and pass it down when I get in." I handed Horace the lantern. Then I swung my legs into the hole and dropped down inside. "Give me the lantern."

104

I reached out for it and he handed it to me, the little specks of light darting around as I pulled it down inside under the sailcloth roof. The light shone through the cloth and anybody who came by would know somebody was moving around in there.

I shone the light on the sleeping person. It was her, all right, lying facedown. I kneeled over her and shook her by the shoulder. She didn't wake up; she just sort of rattled there. I figured she was drunk, which worried me, in case she was too drunk to remember about Ma. So I gave her cheek a little pat, like a soft slap, and as soon as I did I realized that her face was cold. My stomach jumped. I held the lantern down closer to her face. It was turned pretty far down, so's I couldn't see much of it, but I could see one eye shining in the light. It didn't move or wink in the light. I didn't want to touch her no more, but I had to, just in case she was still alive and maybe could be saved. So I laid my hand on her face again. She was stone cold dead. I jumped for the window hole. The candle in the lantern tipped over and went out. I spun around and tumbled out of the hole into the mud. "She's dead, Horace," I whispered, and we ran for it.

10

Now I was stuck. I didn't know if Ma was down in Canvas Town, or had ever been there, or if the sick woman had made the whole story up just to get the money. I was having the hardest time about the whole thing. Ma might be anywhere: a prison ship, a prison, Canvas Town, or somewheres altogether different.

There was one other thing, too: She might be dead. I'd been trying not to think of that, but after seeing the dead woman it came to me that in war a lot of awful things happened to people. Ma could have been killed back there in Groton, somehow, and got buried in a common grave along with Pa. Or she could have got put in a prison ship and took sick and died even before I left Newfield to look for her. Or she could have got to Canvas Town and got murdered there. I just didn't have any idea where to look for her anymore. I was plain stuck.

There wasn't nothing I could do except to feel lucky that I'd got regular meals and a warm place to sleep, which so many around New York didn't have. The city was in bad shape. It'd been occupied by the British for six years, since 1776, when I was a little girl. Food was short, firewood was short, water was short, too. They'd started washing their clothes in Freshwater Pond, and garbage had got into it, drifting in from the swamps where they'd dumped it. But at the tavern we generally had enough to eat, enough firewood, and good water from our own wells.

That was because it was the best tavern in New York, and the British officers saw to it that Mr. Fraunces got what he needed to keep it going. They still didn't have much to do but drill the troops every once in a while. They was bargaining for the end of the war, but everybody said it was going to take a long time, months maybe, to get it settled. Meanwhile the British sat in New York.

Like I said, Mr. Fraunces was a mystery. I couldn't tell for sure if he was black like me, or something else, and I couldn't tell for sure whose side he was on, the British or ours. Uncle Jack had said that he was on the American side. But he was polite to the British, and when they was around, he said things like the rebels was scoundrels and ought to be hanged and such. But maybe he was just saying them things so's the British wouldn't take away his tavern.

One thing that I found mighty instructive was being a boy for a change. If Horace had known I was a girl he'd have always been pushing me around—Willy, do this, do that, fetch me my dinner, see if them chickens have enough water. That was the way Pa treated my Ma. It was his right. He loved her, but he had a duty to command her, too, and she had a duty to obey. It would have been the same with Horace. We wasn't married or anything, and he didn't have no real rights over me, but he'd have taken them, just the same. It was a reason for not letting on to Horace I was a girl. Oh, I didn't want to stay a boy all the rest of my life. I didn't feel like a boy, I felt like a girl. But I was going to be kind of sorry to go back to being a girl and get pushed around by boys again.

I still had in my mind to get Horace to write me a letter to Aunt Betsy, if it was really true that he was such a prince at writing as he said he was. To hear him tell it, he could do the hardest kind of sums in his head like lightning. And spell: why, according to Horace he could spell out the longest words and never make a mistake once. He just amazed his teachers, he said. There wasn't nothing more they could teach him, they told Mr. Fraunces, which was why he didn't go to school anymore.

But the question was how to get the letter up there. So when I got a chance I went around to Mr. Fraunces' office and knocked on his door. He told me to come in and I stood in front of his polished desk amongst the glass bookshelves and polished sconces.

"Sir, I'd like to get word to my Aunt Betsy that I ain't dead or anything."

"She's in Stratford?" he said.

"In Newfield, sir. It's part of Stratford."

He thought about it for a minute. "You can't write, can you, Willy?"

"No, sir, but Horace, he said he'd do it. He said he was a prince at spelling."

Mr. Fraunces smiled, which gave me some idea of it. "Well, he'll manage somehow, I expect." He thought some more. Finally said, "There is a young Connecticut man named Elizur Goodrich in Greenwich arranging for an exchange of some prisoners with the British. Greenwich is just a few miles up the North River. I think you might find them at Richmond Hill. I'm sure he'd be willing to take a letter out and leave it nearby when he gets home. Horace is going up Manhattan soon after a load of hay. He can go through Greenwich and if you ride up with him, you could see if somebody will take your letter for you."

So it was settled, and that night, after we finished our suppers, Horace sneaked a piece of paper that they used for writing out bills on, borrowed a quill from the accounts keeper, and we sat at the little table in the kitchen and worked it out.

I said, "Say, 'Dear Aunt Betsy, I'm living down in—' "

"Hold it, not so blamed fast," Horace said. He'd got himself folded so far over, his nose was nearly touching the paper, and I was afraid he'd stab himself in the

110

eyeball with the quill. He was working out the letters like a man scratching on glass.

"I thought you was a prince at writing, Horace."

"I am," he said. "The only thing is, I sprained my wrist this afternoon combing the horse and I have to go slow on account of it."

"That explains it, then," I said. So I slowed down and gave him the rest, and this is what it came to:

Der Ant Besty
Im living don her in N.Y. with Mr. Frawnses. Im al rit & in good helth. I hev loked for ma but dont find hir nowere. If you noe where she is rit Mr. Froansuz.

There was a whole lot more I wanted to say, but it took near a half an hour to get this far. Horace was complaining that his wrist hurt something awful and he'd better quit before he did it permanent damage. So he signed it "Love Wily" and we folded it up and waxed it, and then of course Horace had to struggle with the address, complaining the whole way. But finally it was done.

A couple of days later we set out. We followed Greenwich Road along the North River. It was a beautiful sunshiny Indian summer morning, with the birds peeping, the low rustle of the river against the shore, the clumping of the horse's hooves and the wagon complaining. There wasn't much of a breeze, and it was going to be hot when the sun got high.

111

We passed through some farmland, and after a couple of miles we came to Greenwich—some small houses here and there, and amongst them a few grand ones. We didn't have no trouble finding Richmond Hill. It was the grandest house of them all, with a fence around it and a great long drive going up to it. We parked the wagon and I walked up around to the back and asked for Mr. Goodrich. By and by a black man came out. He said he was Mr. Goodrich's servant and that Mr. Goodrich was too busy to bother with an ignorant nigger boy. So to soften his heart I explained about Pa getting killed at Fort Griswold and Ma going off, and finally he said he would find Mr. Goodrich.

I waited around for a while, and then out came a white man. He was real young, in his twenties, and dressed up mighty fine in a ruffled shirt and silver buckles at his knees. "You're the boy who was at Fort Griswold?" he said.

I could see that he thought I'd been in the fighting, and I decided there wasn't no harm in letting him think that. "Yes, sir," I said.

He gave me a sharp look. "You must have been pretty young to be fighting."

"I wasn't supposed to be there," I said. "I went up with my Pa to take the horse back and I got stuck."

He thought about that for a minute. Then he said, "Who's your Pa?"

"Jordan Freeman, sir."

"Ah, yes," he said. "I remember the name. He was killed, wasn't he?"

112

"Yes, sir," I said. "I saw it happen."

He nodded and pursed his lips and I could tell he was sorry for me. "Well, all right, then," he said. "Give me the letter. I'll take it back to Connecticut with me and leave it off."

"Thank you, sir," I said. "That's mighty good of you." I handed him the letter.

He took a quick look at it to see where it was going. "Arabus? Jack Arabus?"

"Yes, sir," I said. "He's my uncle."

"I know Jack," he said. "He sails with Captain Ivers —or he used to. They take me from Norwalk to New Haven and back on the *Junius Brutus* on my way to and from Yale. Is he still in the army?"

"I reckon so, sir," I said. "Unless he got killed."

He nodded again. "You have a very patriotic family, I see. Yes, I'll take the letter for you." He went back into the house and I skipped on out of there.

Then we clumped on out to the farm where we was to get the hay. It was across a little river called Turtle Creek. It was a mighty pretty sight, that river running through meadows, and a line of trees along the banks. We got off the wagon, and I pushed and Horace pulled at the horses to get them across. There wasn't no clouds at all, and it was hot work. Then we got out to the farm and loaded up the hay. That was even hotter work. We finished around noon. The farmer gave us some biscuits and cider and then we turned around and started back. Soon we came to Turtle Creek again, running along through the meadows.

113

"I'd sure like to have a swim and cool down," Horace said.

I wasn't too pleased by that idea. "We ain't supposed to fool around, Horace. We're supposed to head right back."

He frowned. "I reckon so," he said.

So we got down off the wagon and pulled and heaved it across. Of course it was loaded down with a ton of hay now. It took us a good fifteen minutes to get it across, and we was pretty well sweated up when we got finished.

Horace stood on the bank, looking down at the cool, running water, hearing it gurgle. "Well, I *am* going to have a swim," he said. "Mr. Fraunces, he'd say so himself. He'd say, 'Boys, it's a mighty hot day, just climb in the water and cool yourself down.'"

I was worried. I could see that he was determined to do it. "Mr. Fraunces wouldn't say no such thing, Horace. He'd say for us to get on back to the tavern as quick as we could clump it."

"How's he going to know, unless you plan to tell him, Willy?"

"Well, no, I wouldn't do that."

"I'm going to do it," he said.

I was pretty anxious. "You'll like to freeze to death going home in wet britches," I said.

He gave me a look. "I ain't going to swim in my clothes, you idiot."

"Oh," I said. "Well, I don't feel much like swimming. Maybe I'll just go out in that field and see if the

114

blueberries is ripe. You just go ahead and have your swim."

"Blueberries?" he said. "Why, what's the matter with you, Willy? Blueberries is long gone."

"Grapes is what I meant to say." I could feel myself getting hot and blushy.

He knew something was wrong and he gave me another funny look. "Come on," he said. "Come on swimming with me."

"I think I'm coming down with a cold," I said.

"You ain't got no cold, Willy," he said.

"All right," I said, "I'll admit it. I don't know how to swim." That was a lie. I could swim as good as anybody. My Pa taught me when I was little.

"Oh, there ain't nothing to swimming," Horace said. "I'll teach you. I'm a wonderful swimmer. Whenever somebody got out too far in the bay, or their boat went over and it looked bad for them, they'd say, 'Quick, send for Horace at Fraunces Tavern. He'll save them if anyone can.' Oh, I was known for it."

I gave him a squint. "How come they ain't sent for you since I been around?"

"Oh, I pulled a muscle in my shoulder a while back, so's I couldn't swim but with one hand. I *could* swim with one hand, too, but that didn't leave no arm to pull the victim along with, so's I had to give it up, temporary. But the one who took over, he's white. Naturally he doesn't want to be beat out by no nigger, so's he won't let them send for me no more."

"Well, Horace," I said, "you're just too good for me.

You go have your swim and I'll see about them grapes."

"Come on, Willy," he said.

He looked hurt, but he'd have looked a whole lot worse if he'd seen me with my clothes off. "No, Horace, it'll just make my cold worse." So I walked out into the field pretending I was looking for grapes. After a few minutes I stood still and listened. Sure enough, I could hear him splashing away down there. The grapes was just come ripe, and I collected up a pretty good bunch in my hat. The sun was warm on my back and the grapes smelled so sweet I couldn't keep from eating some, even though I knew I ought to share them with Horace. Then I realized quite a bit of time had gone along, and we was likely to be late getting back.

I raised up my head and shouted, "Horace, ain't you never coming out?" He didn't answer, and I figured he couldn't hear me at the distance splashing around in the water. I folded the hat over so's the grapes wouldn't fall out, and then I trotted back across the field, and slipped up behind the wagon, where I wouldn't see him. "Horace, it's getting late," I hollered.

There was no answer, and I didn't hear no splashing, neither. Suddenly I began to wonder if he'd drowned or something. I raised up my head from behind the wagon a little. I could see some of the stream, but no Horace. I raised up a little more, and here came Horace up the creek bank stark naked.

116

I squeezed my eyes shut, dropped the hatful of grapes onto the ground, and ran back out toward the field.

"Hey, Willy," he shouted. "Where're you running to?"

I didn't turn around, but kept on running. "I lost something out in the field," I shouted.

"I'll help you find it," he shouted, and started running after me. With those long skinny legs of his I wasn't no match for him. I kept on running, trying to think of what to do, and the next thing I knew he was right there beside me.

There wasn't no point in running no more, so I stopped and faced him, sort of gazing off up into the sky, like I was watching for birds. "You just go back and get dressed, Horace," I said. "I'll find it myself."

"I ain't dried off yet," he said. He dropped down into the grass and sat there, and I went on looking for birds. "What'd you lose, Willy?"

"A pin out of my hat," I said.

"You'll never find it out in this here field, Willy."

"I aim to try," I said. I turned and walked away from him, keeping my eyes stuck to the ground. I figured he'd dry off pretty soon, and I'd just keep looking for the pin until he did.

Then I heard him shout. "Hey, Willy, look what I found."

I sort of half turned, like I was looking at him, but really wasn't. "What is it, Horace?"

117

"Come and see," he shouted.

"I can't," I shouted back. "I'm looking for my hat-pin."

"You ain't going to find that pin in this whole field," he said. "Come and see what I found."

"In a minute," I said. "Why don't you get dressed while you're waiting."

Then he was trotting over straight toward me. There wasn't any way to get out of it now. "Willy," he said, "what's the matter with you today? You're acting mighty strange. You don't want to go swimming, you don't want to do nothing with me."

I was looking up at the birds again. "Horace, I can't do none of them things with you unless you put your clothes on. I ain't a boy, I'm a girl."

I snuck a look down from the birds at him. His whole face seemed to go in six directions at once, with his chin heading south, one eye going east and the other north and his nose sliding around among them trying to make up its mind.

"Willy, you're a girl?"

"I sure am," I said. "I've been one all along." And the next thing I knew he was racing back across the field to the wagon. I gave him a couple of minutes to get dressed and then I walked slowly over there. We stood by the wagon, looking at each other, then we looked away, then we looked at each other again. Finally I said, "I'm sorry I fooled you all this time, Horace, but Mr. Fraunces, he said it was better if nobody knew."

118

"You could have told *me* at least." He was pretty down about it.

"Well, I reckon I should have," I said. "I told you now, anyway."

"That's something, anyways," he said. He was pretty gloomy about it, and angry, too.

"What's so terrible about me being a girl?" I said. "It ain't that awful."

He climbed up onto the seat of the wagon. "It's a mighty big surprise," he said. "It'll take some getting used to."

We didn't say much on the way home. I felt kind of ashamed I'd fooled him so long, but I'd made up my mind there wasn't no reason to be ashamed I was a girl.

WINTER CAME, MIGHTY hard for everybody. Food was short and firewood was short and about everything else was short, too. I worked at the tavern and hunted around town for Ma. The British had so many American soldiers in prison they had to use churches for them, and sugar houses, too, which was empty because there wasn't any sugar coming in from the West Indies. I went around to the prisons and asked the guards if there was any black women inside. But there never was; leastwise they said there wasn't.

But I kept getting that picture in my mind of coming across Ma, just like that, and so when I had the chance, I walked in the streets, looking. I even went back to Canvas Town a couple of times to look.

Meanwhile I'd made it up with Horace for turning

out to be a girl. The first thing he did was to say that I couldn't stay in the barn loft with him anymore. It wasn't right, he said, for a boy and a girl that was nearly growed to sleep together like that. But I didn't like being shoved off like that; it made me mad. I told him lots of times grown men and women who wasn't married had to sleep in the same bed, when there wasn't beds enough to go around, and if he didn't like it, *he* could find some other place to sleep.

But to tell the truth, it made me feel a little funny. We was just friends, and all, but still. So I tried to be careful about how I dressed and undressed. Of course, I didn't have to wear the milking britches no more; one of the cooks got hold of a dress for me. Usually I woke up in the morning before Horace did, and quietly slipped into my clothes. But one morning I happened to glance over at him when I was putting on my dress, and I saw one of his eyes was open. That night I took a horse blanket and slung it over one of the beams in the loft, so's it hung down to the hay. "What's that for, Willy?" Horace said.

"I saw you peeking this morning."

"I wasn't," he said. "I never did." But I noticed that he was blushing red as a baked apple and twisting himself up like a snake, and it gave me the idea that he'd been doing a fair amount of peeking all along.

But finally Horace got used to me being a girl. He left off cursing in front of me and was more polite, but every now and then, if he dropped a board on his foot, or mashed his finger in a door, he'd forget and rip off a string of curses that'd singe the hair off a cowhide. Then he'd remember and look at me sheepish and say he was sorry. I'd tell him there wasn't no point in being sorry, he'd been talking like that in front of me for months. But he'd still look sheepish.

So the winter went along, with everything short. Seventeen eighty-two rolled around. In March the story came that Lord North, the Prime Minister of England who'd been in favor of the war, was out, and the new one coming in would settle the thing and take the British troops back home. In April they began having meetings in Paris between the British, the Americans, and the French, who'd helped the Americans in the war, to work out a peace treaty. Spring was coming, too, and everybody was cheered up a good deal. But it turned out to be a hot, dry summer, and water was shorter than ever. Our wells at the tavern held up, but we had to be careful with it. We was all so impatient for the British to leave, so they'd let the prisoners out. But the whole thing went slow as molasses. Even though they'd been meeting in Paris for months, they didn't get down to real negotiations until September, and it wasn't until November that they signed the first articles of peace.

But aside from still missing Ma, I was pretty content. I liked working at the tavern. It was a lot more interesting than milking Ma's cow or scrubbing Mrs. Ivers's floors. And I liked the people. Mr. Fraunces, he was good to his help so long as they did their work, and I got on with the cooks. So far as Horace was concerned, that was a bit of a puzzle. I didn't exactly know what I felt about him. I wasn't thirteen anymore, I was going on for fifteen. He liked me, I knew that, because if he was in the barn and he saw me come out of the kitchen to pump water, sure enough, about two minutes later he'd come sauntering out, trying to look as if he had a lot of important things on his mind, but wasn't in no rush to decide them, and start giving me orders. It wasn't anything very much, just little things. Like he'd say, "Willy, I've got to go somewheres for Mr. Fraunces, you see to the water for the cook." Or he'd say, "Willy, I ain't got time to mess with them chickens today, you'll have to do it."

He wouldn't have said none of those things before. It might have worked out the same, but he'd have more likely said, "Willy, I've got to go somewheres for Mr. Fraunces. If you do the water today, I'll do it tomorrow." Something more fair and even. But now it was like his time was more important than mine. He couldn't fritter time away, but it didn't so much matter if I did. I don't mean that he tried to lord it over me all the time: he knew better than that. It was mostly little things. Oh, it made me mighty argumentative when he gave me orders like that, and I'd answer him right back, "You ain't my boss, Horace." I liked him, but sometimes he made me mad.

Winter came. In February the British finally proclaimed the end of the fighting, and after that there wasn't no more skirmishing. But still the British troops

124

didn't go. Oh, I was impatient. I didn't know for sure that Ma was in prison somewhere, but it was the likeliest thing. The truth was, though, it had been so long since I'd seen her I couldn't hardly remember what she looked like. I still kept getting this picture in my head of her coming along the street and us hugging and all that, but the picture wasn't so clear anymore. It had been coming up to two years since the fighting at Fort Griswold. Living back there in Groton seemed like another life, and the old me was another person. I missed Ma and sometimes when I remembered Pa and saw that bayonet slide in and him fling his arms out like that I'd get low and would want to go off by myself and not to talk to anybody. But mostly I didn't think about them things. My life now was the tavern and Horace and Mr. Fraunces and the cooks and the rest of them I'd got to know.

I'd saved up a little money. Mr. Fraunces, he wasn't one for throwing his money around casual, but he allowed that me and Horace wasn't slaves and we ought to get wages. So he gave us each a shilling a week, which was twelve pence and would buy a quart of molasses or a half pound of cheese. Horace, he was very near with his money. He wouldn't spend it short of his life depending on it. He'd been saving for years, and he'd got over eight pounds put away. He was going to get his own tavern someday. He'd be a waiter first and learn all about the tavern business, then he'd start his own. Mr. Fraunces told him that he had the

125

smartest head for business he'd ever seen, he said. I didn't dispute that. Horace had his ways, but he wasn't no idiot.

I'd saved some, too, but only about a pound. The trouble with me was I had a sweet tooth. Even though New York was occupied, there was sweet things you could buy. In particular Mr. Joseph Corre's shop was dangerous for me. He always had custards there and Jordan almonds and sugar candies and macaroons. Sometimes the cooks would send me over there to fetch tarts or cakes for the tavern. Of course I'd have to stand around and wait while they did up the parcel, with all of them things smelling just so tempting. I'd promise myself I wouldn't buy nothing, and I'd tell myself to go outside and wait while they made the parcel ready. But I never could do it, and in the end I'd spend sixpence on macaroons or some such. They was expensive, too, being as everything was short and prices up. But I couldn't help myself. Then I'd feel bad about wasting the money and give one of the macaroons to Horace. So he came out a winner no matter what.

March came, and the rumors got stronger and stronger that they was going to end the war once and for all and let the prisoners out. Of course most of the people in the city was loyalists and they was feeling mighty bad. Here they'd gone and stuck up for the British and the king and fought for them and suffered, and now the British had given the whole thing up. The loyalists, they didn't know what they was going to do.

Some of them had the idea of going to England and starting over there, but most of them figured they'd go up to Canada, if they could get the British Parliament to give them land up there. Oh, there wasn't too much jollity in the tavern anymore. The loyalists and the British officers, too, who came in were low as could be. There was a lot of stories going around that some of the loyalists had shot themselves, or hanged themselves, or flung themselves in the river and drowned.

And then one day, early in April, the rumor swept around like a bullet that it *was* over and the prisoners would all be out in a day or two. I was so excited I could hardly stand it. I kept waking up at night with my heart racing, and I wasn't no use at all around the kitchen, because I kept seeing Ma coming along, and couldn't remember what I was doing. I don't know how long I could have stood it, but two or three days later in the middle of the morning Mr. Fraunces came into the kitchen with a big smile on his face and said, "It's over. They've signed it."

Well, we flung up our arms and let out a cheer. We'd won at last. I guess even the loyalists was glad to have it done with, even if they'd lost. And a lot of people, they'd never cared one way or another whether we was ruled by British or Americans, just so long as they could hold on to their property and live their own lives.

Then Mr. Fraunces looked at me. "Willy, they're bringing the prisoners in from the prison ships. Go on down there and see if you can find her."

I didn't wait. I flung on my hat and raced out of there over Dock Street and Water Street to the wharf on the East River. The streets was full of people rushing here and there, some of them looking happy and cheering, some of them mighty worried.

Finally I reached the dock. There was already a lot of prisoners there. They was standing there hugging each other, or so weak they couldn't walk and was lying down, or crawling because their feet was ruined. Out in the water there was boats coming in with more of them. There was British officers there shouting for them to move along. They wasn't doing nothing for them. They was just pushing them off the dock so's they could unload another batch. Oh, it was a terrible sight. They was all so thin from starvation and their clothes all torn and a lot of them sick with sores on their faces, or flushed with fever, or quivering so hard from the ague it seemed they'd shake apart.

After a bit they began to spread off away from the dock. The ones with frostbitten feet couldn't stand at all. I heard later that some of them crawled on their hands and knees all the way to Virginia, where their homes was.

I began running up and down the dock, looking everywhere. I was scared that Ma'd come off the boat and walk away before I could see her. I went up and down the dock twice and didn't see her. So I went to the end of the wharf where the prisoners was landing, and stood there, and waited. I stood there all morning, watching boatload after boatload come in. But she wasn't on any of them.

So I began asking; I went from this one to the next one: did they know of any black woman who was on the prison ships? No, they said, they'd heard a story that there was some women on one of the prison ships, but they'd never seen any themselves. The boatloads kept coming in and I kept asking and all I heard was the same thing: Nobody'd ever seen any women on the prison ships.

It got toward nightfall, with the sun going down over the town and the dark coming up in the rivers. The shadows of the buildings fell across me. The boats kept coming and going and I kept on watching and then I noticed that the boats wasn't going back to the prison ships after they unloaded; they was staying tied up at the dock. Finally there was just one more boat coming in. It tied up, and unloaded the prisoners. I didn't see Ma anywheres among them. The prisoners come onto the dock and went slowly off to town; and then the British officers went off, and finally I was standing there on the dock all alone, with the night coming down around me, and I put my hands over my face and I began to cry, with my shoulders shaking and the tears leaking out through my fingers. I'd waited two years for the war to be over so I could find her. Wasn't I ever going to see my Ma?

Finally I got myself to stop crying and walked back to the tavern. Horace and the cooks, they saw how I looked and didn't say much, but left me alone, and I went into the barn loft. I couldn't fall asleep. I lay there on my back, staring up through the dark, trying to remember what Ma looked like. But I couldn't—I couldn't get a picture of her. All I remembered was that she had chocolate-colored skin and was pretty. And I knew the only thing I could do was forget about her. I wouldn't never see her again. She was gone— dead, or taken back to England, or sold off to the West Indies. Dead, most likely, I figured, for so many of them had died on those prison ships; but whatever had happened to her, I knew I wouldn't never see her no more, so the best thing I could do was forget about her. I was on my own now. It didn't matter how old I was—I was a grown-up now, and had to look out for myself.

Time went on, and still the British didn't leave. Summer came. Loyalists began to go off to Nova Scotia, Canada—a whole fleet of them in April, and more in August, and more in September. The fall came and still the British was there. Finally, around the middle of November, the stories went around that the British was going to leave soon. We waited, just hoping and praying, and then one frosty morning we heard drums beating in the street. We raced out of the kitchen, all of us—me, Horace, the cooks, and every- body—and there out on the street we saw the British redcoats marching down toward the harbor, drums beating, flags waving, looking straight ahead and solemn.

We began to cheer, and in about two minutes the street was full of people cheering the redcoats away. I was standing there, cheering and waving my arms. They marched on and on, and finally they were gone, and there was only the sound of the drums, getting fainter and fainter as they reached the Battery, where they loaded up in ships and sailed away. The terrible war was over.

We went back to the tavern, and I grabbed a bucket and went out into the yard to pump water for washing the breakfast dishes. And I was doing this when a man dressed up in a green suit with silver buckles came out of the kitchen. "I'm looking for Willy Freeman," he said.

He looked familiar to me. "I'm Willy, sir," I said.

He stared at me for a moment. "I thought Willy Freeman was a boy," he said.

I blushed, and suddenly I realized who he was—Mr. Goodrich from Connecticut, who'd taken my letter up to Aunt Betsy. "I *used* to be a boy," I said. "I mean Mr. Fraunces said it would be better if I dressed like a boy."

He thought about that for a minute. "Yes, I see," he said finally. "I have some news for you. I'm afraid it isn't very good news."

"News, sir?"

"I've seen your mother."

"Ma?" Suddenly I felt dizzy. It was like the world had spun around. I'd got things fixed one way in my head, and now they was different. "Ma?"

"Yes," he said. "She's up at the Ivers place in New-field. I'm afraid she's very ill."

"Ma's sick, sir?"

"I'm afraid it's serious," he said.

12

MR. GOODRICH, HE WENT back into the tavern, and I stood there by the pump, dumbstruck. It was the queerest thing; here I'd suddenly got Ma back, and in the next breath I was going to lose her again, for I knew what Mr. Goodrich meant when he said it was serious. It meant that they figured she was going to die.

Oh, I wanted to go up there and save her. I wanted to go up there to give her medicines and feed her right and see that she was warm and comfortable and help her to get better. I couldn't stand her to be dying like that, without me there to look after her.

But if I went up there, Captain Ivers was sure to clap me back into slavery. There wasn't no doubt about that. He'd claim that I was his, and it wouldn't make no difference what I said to anybody because I was just a nigger girl and nobody would pay any attention to me. Oh, how I wished I'd had sense enough to get Pa's papers out of the cupboard in the shack and tote them along with me wherever I went. Oh, how I wished I'd done that.

But it was too late for that. And what was I going to do? Was I going to let Ma die up there and not try to help her, and never see her before she died? Or was I going to go up there and help her, and get myself clapped into slavery?

There wasn't any two ways about it. I had to take the chance and go. So I went back into the tavern, and down to Mr. Fraunces' office, and there was Mr. Goodrich standing by the door, talking with Mr. Fraunces. They looked at me coming along. "Sir—" I said.

"I've heard about it, Willy," Mr. Fraunces said.

"I have to go back there," I said.

"I wish you wouldn't," Mr. Fraunces said. "It's a risk. We may never get you back again."

"I know that, sir," I said. "I know Captain Ivers will try to put me back into slavery. But I have to do it."

Mr. Goodrich gave me a sharp look. "You're free, then?"

"Yes, sir," I said. "When Pa joined up, Colonel Ledyard set Ma and me free, too."

"Do you have papers?"

"No, sir. I didn't think to take them from our cabin."

"That's too bad," Mr. Goodrich said. He took hold of his chin and thought for a minute, and then he said, "I know about Ivers. He'll do it if he can. If you have any trouble along those lines, you come and see me."

"Yes, sir, thank you," I said. "I'll surely do that."

Then Mr. Goodrich said he knew of a ship leaving for Black Rock in two or three days that would let me work my passage that far. I could walk the rest of the way to Newfield pretty easy. So I thanked him for that, too, and it was settled.

I spent the next three days all of a twitch, hardly able to sit still, nor eat anything, nor get on with my work. I was just scared as I could be that Ma would die before I could save her. But then word came that the ship was going to leave in a couple of hours, and I went around to Mr. Fraunces' office to say good-bye.

"I just wanted to thank you for everything you done for me, sir."

He was sitting at his desk, amongst the books and the pewter sconces on the wall. "I've been glad to have you, Willy," he said. "I was hoping you'd be staying with us."

"I wished I was, too," I said. "But I don't know what Ma'll want to do."

"Yes, I understand that," he said. "Just remember, you'll be welcome back anytime."

So he hugged me a little and then he gave me a Spanish dollar and said he hoped I'd saved my wages, and I lied and didn't tell him I'd spent most of it on macaroons. Then I went out into the yard, where Horace was hauling water up from the well.

"I guess I have to say good-bye, Horace," I said. "I'm going directly."

He set down the bucket and looked at me. "Well, good-bye, Willy," he said. "I hope you come back."

"You didn't mind that I turned out to be a girl?"

"I'll admit, it startled me some," he said.

"But you got used to it."

"Yes," he said. "I sort of did."

"It wasn't too bad, was it?"

He thought about it for a minute. "You know, the truth is, Willy, there was times when I was glad you was a girl."

He blushed when he said that, and I blushed and felt like crying a little. So I reached up and put my arms around his neck and hugged him. Then I went after him to kiss him on the lips. He squirmed around but I caught him and gave him a good kiss. "Horace, you ain't much of a kisser," I said.

"I ain't used to being kissed by no boy," he said.

I laughed. "You ain't used to being kissed by no girl, neither," I said.

"Oh, Willy, you'd be amazed by the number of girls that want to kiss me," he said. "I wouldn't never let them. The next thing you know, they want to marry you."

"You got to get married someday, Horace," I said.

"I ain't in no rush," he said. He picked up the water bucket. "Well, maybe you'll come back."

136

"Maybe I will," I said.

I went to the dock and got on board the ship. They set me to polishing brass, and after a bit we set off out of New York harbor. I went out on deck and took a look at the city slipping away behind me. I felt mighty sad and lonely. I missed the tavern already, and Horace and Mr. Fraunces and the cooks and the rest of them. Groton wasn't my home no more, nor Captain Ivers's place, even if Ma was there. The tavern was my home now. But even so, I wanted to see Ma about as bad as anything I'd ever wanted, and it scared me that she might die before I got there to save her, if I could.

We sailed all afternoon, and just as dark was coming we pulled into Black Rock harbor and up to one of the wharves that jutted into the water. There was ships there now that the war was over, and the houses was lit up, looking cheerful. But I'd lived in New York for two years, and Black Rock didn't look like much of a place. I got off the ship, asked my way to Newfield, and started off walking, first up the street from the harbor and then into the country along dirt roads. The dark come up full, the sky was clouded over, and there wasn't no stars. Every once in a while I'd stop at a farmhouse and ask if I was going right for Newfield. Pretty soon I was in Stratfield, the next village to Newfield. There I had to rouse the ferryman to take me across the Pequonnock River. And I had to give him twelve coppers to do it.

Even then he grumbled and said it was against the law to carry niggers unless they had a pass, and I'd better be telling the truth, because he'd check with Captain Ivers, sure enough. But he finally took me, anyway.

Once on the other side, I found the little path going back to the house and walked around to the kitchen yard between the house and the barn. But I didn't dare go in until I found out how things was. So I slipped up to the kitchen window and took a look in. The Arabus family was sitting at the table eating stew. Uncle Jack, Aunt Betsy, and Dan. I was surprised at how big Dan was. He'd grown considerable. It was late to be eating dinner, and I knew that Captain Ivers had kept them working a long day. But why was Uncle Jack sitting there with them? The war was over, and he was supposed to be free, and could eat dinner whenever he wanted.

There was no sign of the Iverses, so I rapped on the glass a couple of times with my knuckles. Their heads snapped around. I pressed my face to the window so's they could see me, and in a minute they came boiling out the back door into the kitchen yard. Aunt Betsy hugged me, and Uncle Jack hugged me, and Dan, he sort of circled round and round me, all of us whispering and trying not to make any noise. Aunt Betsy said how I'd grown, and I said how Cousin Dan had grown, and then I said, "How's Ma?"

Uncle Jack looked serious. "She's pretty bad, Willy."

"I got to see her," I said.

"It's risky," Uncle Jack said. "Ivers has been telling

people for two years you ran away from him. He
claims he bought you from Colonel Ledyard just before he was killed."

"It's not true," I said. I was getting angry.

"You'd best not be caught, anyway," Uncle Jack
said. "He's a bad one."

Aunt Betsy touched my arm. "He's trying to put
Jack back into slavery. He says he never promised Jack
his freedom."

"But the law says Uncle Jack is free," I said, too
loud. My trouble was I'd got use to being free.

"Keep your voice down, Willy," Aunt Betsy said.

"Ivers, he ain't much interested in what the law
says," Uncle Jack said. "He's going to keep me in slavery if he can. Now, I know you want to see your Ma,
but it ain't safe here for you."

"I got to see her," I said.

"Let her, Jack," Aunt Betsy said. "She's got to see
her Ma at least once."

That had a terrible sound to it, but I didn't say
anything. We slipped into the kitchen.

Ma was down in the cellar, where the Iverses made
the Arabuses sleep. I went on down the cellar stairs.
Being as it was November, it was cold and damp
down there—cold and damp most of the year, anyway. They'd set up a candle on a board. Ma was lying
on a straw pallet with a blanket over her. The light
flickered across her face. It was thin and pale and
wrinkled, and her hair was thin, too, and gone gray.

139

She wasn't pretty anymore. If I hadn't have known who it was, I would never have recognized her. It hurt awful for me to see her look like that.

She heard me come down and turned to me. "Who's that?" she said in a whispery voice.

"It's me, Ma."

"Willy? It's you, Willy?" She looked like she couldn't hardly believe it.

I went over and crouched beside her. "It's me, Ma." Close up she looked just awful. There was sweat on her face and her eyes were blank, like whoever it was supposed to be behind them had gone away. She seemed like a stranger to me, an old woman who didn't have nothing to do with my Ma. "I'm here now, Ma. I'm going to take care of you."

"You mustn't stay, Willy," she said. "Captain Ivers will catch you. He's trying to catch Jack already."

"Don't worry about me, Ma," I said. "I'm going to take care of you." Strange as she looked, I didn't want to touch her. But I put my hand on her forehead. She was awful hot. "Ma, I'm going to get you a doctor."

She shook her head slowly. "Captain Ivers, he won't allow it," she said in her whispery voice. She closed her eyes. "I'd best just die."

It troubled me that she'd give up so. "No, Ma," I said. "I ain't going to let you die."

She didn't answer, but lay still. I watched. She seemed to be asleep, so I went on upstairs. They were waiting for me. "She's mighty bad," I said. "I've got to get her a doctor."

Uncle Jack shook his head. "Captain Ivers, he won't allow it."

"I can pay for it," I said. "I have my own money." I had the Spanish dollar Mr. Fraunces had given me, and over a pound I'd saved from my wages. Now I wished I'd saved more, but it was too late for that.

"It won't matter," Uncle Jack said. "He says she's going to infect the whole household. He wants us to take her out of here." He stood up. "Now look, Willy, you can't let Ivers catch you here. You best go out and stay in the barn."

So I did that, and Uncle Jack came out with me with a lantern so's it would look like he was seeing to the cow in case the Iverses noticed the light. He got me a horse blanket and a piece of sailcloth to sleep under. Then he sat with me for a minute and told the whole story.

The British had kept Ma on a ship for two years to wash clothes for the officers. After a while she'd got sick with the fever. She was sick for weeks before she got better. But she never really got over it—sometimes better, sometimes worse. Finally, when the peace was signed, the British had to put her off, because they wasn't allowed to take any American slaves away with them. They put her off on Long Island. She got word over to Uncle Jack where she was, and Uncle Jack, he borrowed a sailboat and come and got her. "She was mighty sick, and I didn't know as she'd make the trip across," he said.

Then he told me about the trouble with Captain

141

Ivers. Uncle Jack *was* free; he had his discharge papers and his soldier's notes that was supposed to be good as money, that they'd paid him for fighting for seven years. But Captain Ivers said no, he wasn't free. And Uncle Jack didn't dare run off because he was afraid Ivers would sell Aunt Betsy and Dan down to the West Indies. "I got to figure out a way to get some money to buy them free," he said. "I got to get a fishing boat and earn some cash money."

"Ain't your soldier's notes enough?"

"It ain't certain what they're worth. The Congress don't have no way to raise money to pay them off. All they are now is just paper. I could get maybe a few pounds for them. Not enough to do any good. All I can do now is wait."

Well, it was a terrible thing. It seemed like the black folks was bound to lose, no matter what happened. But I was too tired and worried about Ma to think about it, so I crawled up into the barn loft, snuggled down in the hay under the horse blanket and the sailcloth, and went to sleep.

I woke up at daybreak, and sat there in the barn loft until Dan came out to look after the cow. He climbed up the ladder into the loft and gave me some biscuits, some cheese, and an apple. I was mighty glad to get them. "Ma says to tell you that the Iverses are going off toward suppertime," he said. "You'll get a chance to come in and see your Ma."

I was glad of that. I was bound and determined to get the doctor for her. So I waited, feeling pretty

142

scared and worried, but I worked hard all day to keep my mind off it. Then in the late afternoon I heard Uncle Jack come into the barn and take out the horse; and then I heard voices; and finally I heard the horse go off; and Uncle Jack climbed up the ladder and told me to come down, the Iverses would be gone for a couple of hours. So I climbed down and went into the house and into the cellar.

Ma was lying there with those blank eyes staring up at the ceiling the way she was before, her face pale and sweaty. But she was breathing very hard now, in a sort of raspy way, and I knew she'd got worse in the night.

"Ma," I said.

She moved her head around to look at me, but she didn't say anything. "Ma, don't just look at me, say something."

She shook her head. "Willy," she said in a low raspy voice. Then she began to cough and turned away from me again. When she stopped coughing she went back to staring at the ceiling again and breathing hard.

"Ma, I'm going to get the doctor." She didn't say anything, but shook her head.

"I'm going to get him, Ma."

Now she slowly turned her head to look at me, as if she wasn't sure it was worth the trouble. "It ain't no use, Willy," she whispered.

I jumped up. She was going to die for sure if I didn't get some medicine. "Ma, I'm going for the doctor."

She reached out to touch me, but I dashed for the stairs and raced up. I didn't know how much it would cost, but I figured I had enough. Uncle Jack and Aunt Betsy and Dan was in the kitchen, waiting for me.

"I got to get the doctor for Ma," I cried.

Uncle Jack shook his head. "Captain Ivers don't want no doctoring for her. He says it's a waste of money."

"I got my own money," I said. "I've been saving my wages."

"The doctor ain't going to come unless Captain Ivers sends for him."

"I got to get him. I got my own money."

"We sent for him a week ago," Uncle Jack said. "He says he can't come if Ivers don't want him."

"He has to come."

I saw what it was: They'd given up on Ma. They figured she couldn't live and there wasn't no sense in causing trouble over it. "I'm going to save her," I said.

"No, you ain't," Uncle Jack said. "Nobody—" Aunt Betsy give him a look. "You just stay right here, Willy," he said.

I never felt so argumentative before in my life, but this time I wasn't going to argue. "Uncle Jack, I'm going. You aren't going to tell me to let my Ma die."

Uncle Jack let his breath out in a long sigh. "Well, I reckon you got a right to try to save her if you want."

So they told me where the doctor was, who was Dr. Beach, and off I went as fast as I could through the dark. I followed along the way they said and by and by I saw a light, and then the house loomed up out of the dark. I rang the bell. Dr. Beach's wife came to the door.

"My Ma is real sick," I said. "She needs the doctor."

She shook her head. "He's busy. He can't come now."

"He's got to come," I cried out. "She's going to die."

She thought about it for a minute. Then she said, "Well, come in. I'll see."

I came into a little hall where there was a bench and a rack for coats and a door and nothing else. His wife opened the door. I could see the doctor talking to somebody. She said something to him and then she came out and shut the door. "He'll come out as soon as he can," she said. Then she went away.

So I sat there and waited, feeling scared and sick inside, like I was slowly breaking to pieces in there. The doctor didn't come and I went on waiting and trying to think of prayers, and still he didn't come. Time just went on. The Iverses would be home soon. I sat there for what seemed like hours.

Finally he came out. There was another man with him, and they chatted and then the other man went off and the doctor said to me, "Yes?"

"I'm from Captain Ivers's house, sir. My Ma's there, and she's dying. You got to come, sir." My heart was beating fast.

He looked at me for a minute. Then he shook his head. "I'm afraid I can't."

145

"Can't come?" I stared at him, confused. "I can pay," I said. "I have my own money."

"It isn't that," he said. "Captain Ivers doesn't want me."

"But she ain't his Ma," I shouted. "She's mine."

"It's his house," he said. "I can't go into a man's house if he doesn't want me there."

I dropped down on my knees in front of him and the tears began to run down my face. "Please, sir," I said.

He winced like he was hit. Then he said, "I'll give you some medicine. It might help."

"Oh, thank you, sir," I said.

He went into his office and in a minute he came out again with a little vial of powders. "Mix this with rum and give it to her," he said.

I took the vial and reached into my pocket and drew out the Spanish dollar. "I don't want any money," he said.

"Thank you, sir," I said. I tore out of there and ran all the way back to the house. The Iverses were still away. I went around to the kitchen door. "I've got to have some rum," I said.

Aunt Betsy got out a bottle of rum, put some in a cup, and I mixed the powders in. Then I went down into the cellar with it, going as quick as I could without spilling. Aunt Betsy came down behind me. Ma was lying on her back, breathing with that hard, raspy sound. She was just staring at the ceiling, waiting to die.

146

"Ma," I screamed. "Don't do that." I knelt down beside her. "Ma, I have the medicine."

She turned her head to look at me and give me a little smile. "Willy," she said in a soft voice. She reached out her arm to touch me, but just then she had a fit of coughing and put her hand over her mouth.

"Ma, take the medicine."

She looked at me for a little bit as if she was trying to remember something, and then she turned and went back to staring at the ceiling. I put my arm under her head, lifted it up a little, and tried to pour some medicine into her mouth. It just went in and then she turned her head a little, coughed, and the medicine sprayed out.

I jumped up and ran upstairs for more rum. Uncle Jack came rushing up behind me. "Willy, stop," he shouted. Captain Ivers was standing in the kitchen. I jerked back when I saw him.

"You," he said in that cold voice.

"Captain Ivers, we got to have the doctor," I shouted. "I can pay for it. I've got my own money."

"You," he said. "You back here?"

I jumped over to him and grabbed him by his jacket. "Oh, God, she's dying, she's dying."

He slapped my hand away from his jacket. I looked at Uncle Jack. His fists was clenched and he was shaking. "Willy," he said in a low voice, "you go back down to your Ma."

I swung around to Captain Ivers again. "She's dying," I hollered. "You're killing her."

147

He didn't answer. Uncle Jack grabbed me by the shoulders and shook me. "Get ahold of yourself, Willy," he said. "Go down to your Ma."

There was tears streaming all down my face and I could hardly see to get down to the cellar. Aunt Betsy was kneeling over Ma, praying. Ma was kind of shaking and rattling and Aunt Betsy had lifted her up and was holding her there.

"Ma," I shouted.

She turned her eyes to me again, looking kind of confused, like she didn't know who I was anymore. "Ma, it's me," I shouted.

"Willy?" she murmured. She tried to reach out her hand to touch me, and then she gave a rattle and died, with her hand stuck out toward me like that.

What I did then I've never been sure. The next thing I remember is being up in the kitchen pounding away at Captain Ivers with my fist. I must have clawed his face, too, because he had big scratches running down his cheeks. I remember seeing the blood oozing out of the scratches and then I felt a bang and heard a crash, and I was lying on the floor and he was standing over me with his whip, just looming up over me, and the whip rising up and starting down. I closed my eyes and the whip ripped across my face, making me cry out.

Then I heard a smack. The captain shouted and Mrs. Ivers began to scream. I opened my eyes. The captain was slumped against the kitchen wall and Uncle Jack was standing over him, his fist clenched.

Captain Ivers was spitting blood out of his mouth and blood was still oozing out of the scratches I'd made on his face.

"Arabus," Captain Ivers said in a hoarse voice, "I'll have you jailed for that."

Uncle Jack had saved me. Captain Ivers would have whipped me half to death. Then Uncle Jack turned, ran out the door, and disappeared into the dark. The next thing I knew Captain Ivers was racing out into the dark after him, with the biggest pistol I ever saw in one hand. Aunt Betsy came dashing up from the cellar. We heard a shout and running feet and suddenly the gun went off as loud as a cannon shot. Aunt Betsy sort of gasped and put her hands over her mouth.

Mrs. Ivers had stopped screaming. "I wouldn't be Jack Arabus for anything," she said. "The captain's going to kill him now for sure, if he ain't dead already." She whirled around and stamped out of the kitchen, and we heard her locking herself into her bedroom.

Aunt Betsy looked at me. I felt just terrible. If it hadn't been for me losing my head and going for Captain Ivers, Uncle Jack wouldn't have done it, no matter what Captain Ivers did. I could see Aunt Betsy was thinking the same thing, too, and I turned my head down.

"I got to do for your Ma," Aunt Betsy said. She went back down the cellar.

Oh, I felt so bad. Ma was dead and Uncle Jack was

149

in bad trouble for hitting a white man. Maybe he was wounded or worse. I wanted to do for Ma myself. But I knew, no matter what, I'd better get myself away from there. Ivers, he was sure to catch me now. There wasn't anybody left to testify that I was free, except maybe Mrs. Ledyard; and she was up in Groton and no use to me.

Dan was standing there, looking mighty confused and worried. I gave him a hug and said, "Tell your Ma I'm sorry for all the trouble I made. I'm going to try to get back down to New York." He said he would, and I hugged him again because I figured it would be a long time before I got to hug anybody again. Then I darted out the kitchen door.

It was starless overhead, and cold, and it looked like it might snow. I stood in the backyard, looking around. Out behind the barn was a field and beyond that a woodlot. I didn't know what was behind the woodlot, but it seemed like the safest place, so I began to run, skirting around the barn and then across a field, until I came to the woods. The leaves was off the trees, which didn't make it too good of a hiding place, but I figured once I was pretty far in they wouldn't be able to see me from the house, anyway. So I went on in, pushing through the brush until I could just barely see the barn and the house through the trees, and then I stopped and crouched down to think. As I did so, something fluttered cold on my cheek. It was starting to snow.

I'd sure made a mess of things. I'd got Uncle Jack in

a lot of trouble, and myself as well. I felt awful that Ma was lying down there in that cold, damp cellar, and I wasn't there to do for her. It hurt me to think of that. But what could I do?

Suddenly I remembered Mr. Goodrich. Hadn't he said he'd help me if I needed it? Yes, he'd said it. But would he?

I was thinking about that, when I heard something from somewhere down by the house. My heart started to beat fast. I wondered if I ought to run off through the woods. I watched the house, and in a minute I saw Captain Ivers, looking small in the distance, come running out of the house and into the barn. I went on watching and a couple of minutes later he came riding out on his horse and galloped away.

What did that mean? Had Uncle Jack got away? I stood there, not knowing what to do. After a minute it came to me that maybe, if Captain Ivers stayed away for a while, I could take a chance on slipping back to the house and see Ma buried proper. But suppose Captain Ivers came back and caught me there? I'd end up in the West Indies for sure.

And suppose I went into New Haven looking for Mr. Goodrich and Ivers caught me *there*. I'd end up in the West Indies, too. There wasn't no doubt about it, the best thing would be to clear out as fast as I could. If I could steal a boat somewhere, I could sail back down to New York. That was going to be risky, but trying to walk down through woods and fields would

151

be riskier, because of being spotted by farmers and such. In a boat I could cross over to the Long Island side of the Sound and go along there.

But where was I going to find a boat? Then a thought came to me. Captain Ivers had a dory down by his dock. Maybe nobody was watching the dory.

So I crept back into the woods a bit, and then began to scramble off through the brush and branches toward the east, figuring on circling around to the water, and then coming up to the dock from the opposite direction. Of course, I didn't know what I'd run into—fields, or more woods, or a road, or what—but there was only one way to find out. It was snowing heavier now and I was fearful cold.

I pushed on through and after a while the woods ended and I came to a field. I crouched down there and studied it. There was a barn in the middle of the field. I'd have to make a dash for it. I figured I'd be all right, because the falling snow would make me hard to see.

And then all at once it came to me that Aunt Betsy and Dan was going to have to go out into that snow all by themselves and bury Ma. She was my Ma, and I'd left somebody else to do for her. And on top of it, I'd got Uncle Jack into a heap of trouble, and here I was just running off and leaving them all to get out of it as best as they could. It was wrong, and I knew it.

But if I went back to Iverses' they'd sure as anything tie me up or send for the constable to keep me till the captain could sell me off. I couldn't save Ma. I couldn't do nothing for Uncle Jack—or could I? If Mr. Goodrich could help me, maybe he could help Uncle Jack. At least I should tell Aunt Betsy about Mr. Goodrich.

I felt so ashamed of myself I could hardly stand it. So I turned and scrambled back through the brush and the branches the way I came, and in a few minutes I was back at the edge of the field looking toward the Ivers house and the barn. The snow was coming down steady now, and I knew we was in for a good storm.

I ran out of the woods and across the field through the falling snow to the house. When I got to the kitchen, I crouched down by the window and peered in. There wasn't nobody there. I figured Aunt Betsy was down in the cellar with Ma. I slipped into the kitchen and opened the cellar door. There was a little light coming up from below. I went on down. Aunt Betsy and Dan was there in the chill damp, kneeling beside Ma and praying. The candlelight flickered across their faces, cutting them up into orange and brown patches, and flickered on Ma's face, gray and thin and blank. I knelt down beside them to pray myself, but the tears began to leak out of my eyes and I couldn't think of no words except please God, please God, please God. Upstairs overhead I could hear Mrs. Ivers tromping around the keeping room, but I knew she wouldn't dare come down to the cellar where there was a dead body; she was too scared.

Then Aunt Betsy started in singing "Old Hundred" in a low voice and Dan and I joined in. After we was finished we said the Lord's Prayer, and that was the best we could do for Ma. Aunt Betsy pulled the blanket over her face, and I knew it was the last time I'd see her. "We got to bury her right away," Aunt Betsy said. "Before the ground freezes any deeper."

"It's snowing," I said.

"It figured to snow," Aunt Betsy said. "What are you aiming to do now, Willy? You can't stay here."

"What's going to happen to Uncle Jack if they catch him?" I said. We were talking in low voices so's Mrs. Ivers wouldn't hear.

She looked at me, mighty somber, the orange and brown patches sliding around her face as the candle flickered. "He'll sell him off now," she said. "He'll steal his soldier's notes and sell him off to the West Indies."

"But he's got his discharge papers."

"He ain't got them with him," she said. "They're right down here, hidden." She looked grim. "Well, they ain't caught him yet, so far as we know. We'd best get your Ma buried before the snow gets too deep."

We wrapped her up in the blanket, and Aunt Betsy sent Dan up for a needle and thread and we sewed the blanket up around her. Dan stayed at the top of the cellar stairs to watch for Mrs. Ivers, and Aunt Betsy and I carried Ma up. She didn't weigh hardly anything; I could have carried her myself. I felt so sorry

154

for her, to be so little. We left Dan in the kitchen, so's to come running to warn us if Captain Ivers came back. Aunt Betsy collected a pick and a shovel from the barn. She gave them to me and she picked up Ma, sewed up in that blanket, and carried her like a baby out to the woodlot. We didn't want to bury her in the field where they would be plowing in the spring, even though they wasn't likely to plow so deep as to disturb a body. We found a place that was partly cleared, and began to dig.

The snow was coming down steady now, like a flurry of cream. We went on digging. Aunt Betsy swung the pick to chop the dirt loose and I shoveled it out; and then we switched around. And all the time Ma lay there sewed up in the blanket, with the snow gradually covering over her. It gave me a queer feeling to think of her lying there, cold and stiff—not a person anymore, just nothing at all. I tried not to think about it, but went on digging.

It took us an hour to get down three feet. We knew we ought to go down six feet, but we wasn't likely to. "Another foot'll be enough," Aunt Betsy said. And we'd got a good deal of that done when suddenly we heard footsteps and saw Dan come running across the field. He came into the woods, breathing hard. "They caught Pa," he said.

We stopped digging. "They caught him?"

"Some man just come running up and told Mrs. Ivers that they'd caught Pa and the captain wouldn't be home tonight, but would be staying in New Haven to sell him off. They got him locked up in jail."

Aunt Betsy looked like death. She leaned her arm against a tree. "We got to get his discharge papers to him. It's the only thing that'll save him."

"I'll take them to him."

She looked at me. "You daren't, Willy. Soon as Ivers sees you he'll lock you up and sell you off, too."

I thought for a minute. Then I remembered. "Mr. Goodrich, he'll do it. He's a lawyer, he'll know what to do."

She stared out across the woods to the house. "It's a mighty big risk, Willy."

I knew that, but I had to take the chance. Uncle Jack had got himself in all this trouble saving me from a flogging. I wouldn't have to go nowheres near Captain Ivers. All I had to do was give Mr. Goodrich the papers. He'd know what to do. "I'll do it anyway," I said.

She left off gazing across the field. "It's our only chance," she said. She sent Dan back to the house to get the papers from where they was hidden in the cellar, and we went back to digging. Just about the time Dan came back with the papers we'd got the grave deep enough. We picked up Ma and set her down in the grave. We pushed the dirt back in, and tamped it down, and then we piled up some rocks on top so no animals could dig down, and we'd know where the grave was. After we was all finished, we knelt down and said the Lord's Prayer again. Then Aunt Betsy told me how to get to New Haven—across the woodlot to the Milford Highway, and along to the Housatonic River and across that, and through Milford on the other side into New Haven. The hard part was going to be getting across the river; most ferrymen wouldn't be so lax as the last one. The law was they couldn't carry no black folks without a pass, but I figured I'd work out a way. Aunt Betsy gave me a heavy cloak; I remembered how I'd taken her old one. I put the papers in my shirt and hugged Aunt Betsy and hugged Dan, and set off through the trees.

The snow was coming down hard now, blowing cold into my face. I was just as glad of it, because anybody who came along wouldn't be able to see me very well. I figured if I kept moving pretty brisk I'd stay warm enough. I pushed on through the woodlot, and then across the field beyond, through the orchard beyond that, and onto the Milford Highway. Then I put my head down and just plowed along, as fast as I could go. The snow was flinging itself at me and sometimes the wind would gust up and toss a great patch of flakes in my face, so's I'd have to stop and turn away. The snow was making a whooshing noise and muffling other sounds, and I knew I wouldn't be able to hear anybody coming along until they was near on top of me. That worried me, and I tried to keep looking around. Looking behind wasn't so bad, but it wasn't easy looking straight forward, with the snow blowing direct into my face. There wasn't nothing to do but push along, and by and by I came to the Housatonic River.

The snow was whipping around the ferryman's house, but I could see a light on inside. There was a wharf sticking into the river with three or four rowboats of different sizes tied up to it. I went to the ferryman's house and knocked. In a minute the door opened and an old man came out, holding a pot of mulled cider. He hadn't shaved for a while and his face was covered with white hairs.

"Yes?" he said.

The steam coming up from the mulled cider smelled so warm and sweet I could hardly stand it, I was so cold and wet. Just looking at him I knew he wasn't going out in a snow storm for no nigger. "Sir, did Captain Ivers come along here a while ago?"

"What business is it of yours?"

"I got this paper I got to give to him," I said. "He sent for it. That big nigger of his is locked up in New Haven and Captain Ivers needs the paper."

He squinted at me. He didn't fancy going out in that storm at all. "You telling the truth?"

"Oh, yes, sir." I reached into my shirt and pulled out the paper. "He needs it right away."

He took a swallow of the mulled cider. The steam came off it into my nose and I could almost taste it going down. "I expect somebody's going to pay for this?" He never even looked at the papers. I reckoned he couldn't read any more'n I could.

"Oh, yes, sir," I said. I reached into my pocket and took out a shilling. He looked at it, like he didn't trust it. Then he put it into his pocket, and we went down to the wharf and he rowed me across.

After that there wasn't nothing to do but keep on walking. It was coming up to dusk, which made me harder to spot. I plowed on, the snow whipping into my face and getting down under my shirt. My feet was soaked, and my clothes was soaked through, too, and I was scared I'd catch the ague, and scared somebody'd catch me, too. But there wasn't nothing to do about that, so I plowed ahead, and by and by the houses began to get closer and closer and soon I was near the center of town.

The streets was mud, but it was frozen and covered with snow and pretty slippery going. I went along between the houses. Some of them was shut up and dark, but in others there was a light going and a red glow from the fire. It looked so cozy and safe in them houses—I wanted to be someplace like that.

Finally I came to a tavern. I went in and asked where Mr. Goodrich lived. They said he lived with a family just a little ways from there.

In a few minutes I was there, and knocking on his door. In a minute a woman opened it. I figured it was his landlady. "I have to see Mr. Goodrich, ma'am."

She looked me up and down. I was so covered with snow and damp you could hardly tell if I was black or white. "It must be mighty important to come out on a night like this."

"Yes, ma'am, it is."

"Well, Mr. Goodrich is very busy. I don't know as I ought to disturb him."

"I walked all the way from Stratford, ma'am."

"Glory," she said. "That's a good ways. You brush yourself off good, now, before you come in. I don't want no water dripping on my floors. I'll go see if he's busy."

"Yes, ma'am," I said. I brushed myself off with my hands and came in. There was a little fire in the fireplace and the room was so warm and cozy I liked to cry. I went over to the fire and stood there dripping on the hearthstone. I wished I could take my clothes off and dry out.

I waited, and then Mr. Goodrich came down, wearing that same green suit he had on before. I guessed, being as he was just starting in as a lawyer, he hadn't made enough money yet to spend on clothes.

He looked at me, puzzled. "Why, it's Willy Freeman," he said. "I didn't expect to see you again so soon."

"Nor me either, sir. But we've got bad trouble." So I told him the whole story, about me coming up from New York, and Ma dying and Captain Ivers flogging me, and Uncle Jack hitting Captain Ivers and getting put in jail. At the end I showed him the paper.

He studied the paper for a minute. Then he looked up at me. "You mean Ivers intends to sell Jack off South?"

"That's what we reckon, sir. He never agreed that

160

Uncle Jack was free. He always wanted to keep him a slave."

Mr. Goodrich shook his head. "He can't do that. That's contrary to the law." He took out his watch and looked at it. "I'm going down to the jailhouse to see your uncle. Want to come?"

"I daren't," I said. "Captain Ivers might be there. He means to stay in New Haven tonight."

"You'll be safe with me. I can just as easily claim you're my slave as he can."

"Still, if you don't mind, sir, I'd rather not take the chance."

He shrugged. "As you like." He put on his hat and his cloak and went out, and as soon as he done that I lay down in front of the fire and fell asleep, even though my clothes was wet and awful uncomfortable.

13

WHEN I WOKE UP, the sun was shining through the small windows of the boardinghouse, bright as could be. I could hear the tink tink of melting snow dripping from the eaves. I raised my head and looked around, trying to make out where I was. Then I remembered.

I stood up. My clothes was pretty well dried, and I felt a lot better than before, but hungry. I could smell biscuits cooking somewhere. And I was thinking about food when Mr. Goodrich came into the room, still wearing that same green suit. I felt kind of sorry for him, that he wasn't rich yet, the way a lawyer was meant to be.

"I saw your uncle last night, Willy," he said. "I'm going to court now to petition for a writ of habeas corpus. I'm going to try to get a hearing on it immediately."

"Habeas corpus?"

"It means that they have to show some good reason for keeping your uncle in jail. I don't think they have any. The only thing that worries me is the possibility of an assault charge. He admits to hitting Ivers."

"That was only for saving me from a beating."

"It'll depend on what the court believes," he said. Then he put on his cloak and hat and went out.

The smell of biscuits was still coming from somewhere, and there was bacon added onto it, too, now. I put my nose up and sniffed, and in a moment I judged the smell was coming from the back of the house. I found my way back, and sure enough, there was a kitchen. The woman who'd let me in the day before had got a pan of meat over the fire, and she was just taking a load of biscuits from the brick oven in the fireplace.

I swallowed hard. "Ma'am," I said, "I'd be glad to work out a couple of them biscuits."

She cocked her head at me.

"You missed your dinner last night, didn't you?"

"I missed pretty near everything yesterday."

"You poor thing," she said. "Well, you set down and eat, and after I get finished feeding my boarders you can help me clean up." So I ate, and then I helped her serve the boarders, which was mostly students at Yale College, and then I started to wash the dishes in a big

wooden tub she had. And I was doing this when Mr.
Goodrich came into the kitchen.

"Dry your hands off, Willy," he said. "We've got to
get back to court in five minutes."

"Sir, I don't dare. Captain Ivers is sure—"

"Don't worry about that," he said. "I may need you
to testify. I think it would be helpful all around if you
came along."

I didn't feel like arguing with Mr. Goodrich, but I
sure didn't want to get into a courtroom with Captain
Ivers. It flashed through my mind that I could just run
off again like I had before. But that wouldn't help
Uncle Jack none, and besides, Mr. Goodrich kind of
left it up to me. I decided that I had to forget whatever Captain Ivers might do to me and do my best to
help Uncle Jack. I'd go along with Mr. Goodrich and
take a chance that he'd save me from Captain Ivers.
So we set off at a good pace down the street and
across a big green with three churches in it and hundreds of little elms and buttonwoods they'd just
planted. Next we came to a row of brick buildings,
which was Yale College. Across the green was the
courthouse with wide steps going up, columns along
the front, and great big windows.

We went up the steps and inside, and down a long
corridor and into the courtroom itself. It was mighty
fancy, a great high room with tall windows around
most of it, a high bench for the judge, and rows of
pews for anybody that was watching. There wasn't too

many people there, but one of them was Uncle Jack, sitting in a pew, with manacles on his wrists and a guard on either side of him. And a little farther down the pew was Captain Ivers. There was a man sitting next to him done up in a fancy suit. I figured he was Captain Ivers's lawyer.

One look at Captain Ivers and all I wanted to do was skedaddle out of there, but Mr. Goodrich marched right to the front and plunked himself down about two feet from Captain Ivers. There wasn't nothing I could do but march along behind him and plunk myself down there, too. Then the judge came in and we all stood up; and that was when Captain Ivers spotted me. "Well," he said. "Look who's turned up." A little smile twisted his lips.

The judge told us to sit down. He looked to be in his fifties. His name was James Wadsworth, Mr. Goodrich said. The judge wore spectacles and had a great shock of hair, like a lion.

So they started up. Captain Ivers stood to one side with his lawyer, whose name was Mr. Chauncy, and Uncle Jack stood to the other side with Mr. Goodrich.

Captain Ivers had a bill of sale for when he'd bought Jack years before. His lawyer read it out, and then the judge asked for it and read it over to himself, peering through his spectacles.

Mr. Goodrich stepped forward. He had some papers that he read off about all the battles Uncle Jack was in and the names of his officers. He read that out, and then the judge asked for the papers and sat at his desk reading them over and frowning.

"Under the law," Mr. Goodrich said, "no slaves were permitted to enlist, Your Honor. Captain Ivers consented to my client's enlistment. Indeed Ivers sent Arabus as his substitute in the first place. It is therefore implicit that Captain Ivers manumitted my client at that time. I would point out further that Captain Ivers kept the state bounty afforded to a slave owner who frees a slave in order to allow him to enlist."

The judge took off his spectacles and leaned forward. "How do you respond to that, Mr. Chauncy?"

Mr. Chauncy stood up. "Your honor, there's a question of assault. Arabus deliberately attacked Captain Ivers with no provocation."

Mr. Goodrich got up, too. "Your honor, I have another client here besides Jack Arabus. Her name is Wilhelmina Freeman and she wishes to lodge an assault charge against Captain Thomas Ivers."

"What nonsense is that?" Captain Ivers shouted. "I've a right to beat my niggers."

"Your honor, my client is a free black and as such a citizen of the state of Connecticut, and under the protection of our laws. Yesterday morning Captain Ivers lashed her with no provocation."

"No provocation?" Captain Ivers shouted. "No provocation? She attacked me." The judge held up his hand. He looked at Captain Ivers, and then at me, and back to Captain Ivers. Then he said, "This girl at-

167

tacked you, Captain? Why, she's half your size." He waved to me. "Come here, Wilhelmina, and let's hear your side of it."

So I told the whole story: about Captain Ivers not letting Ma have any doctoring, and her dying, and Captain Ivers lashing me, and I didn't leave none of it out, even the part about me losing control of myself and scratching his face. And when I was finished, the judge said, "Captain Ivers, did you really take a lash to this girl here while her mother was dying?"

Captain Ivers stood there staring at the judge with that cold face still as a frozen pond, but he didn't say anything. Then Mr. Goodrich said, "Unless Captain Ivers can produce a bill of sale for Willy, she's free." He stared at Captain Ivers, and Captain Ivers stared back. Then Mr. Goodrich said in a soft voice, "Her father was killed fighting for his country and her mother was imprisoned by the British and died from it. And this man, Jack Arabus, spent seven years fighting to protect his country, too. And all the while you sat at home and did business in order to enrich yourself."

Captain Ivers turned to Mr. Goodrich. "Goodrich, you damned little pipsqueak, what do you know about it? Do you take a nigger's word against mine?" He started to go on, but Mr. Chauncy grabbed his arm.

"Your honor," Mr. Chauncy said to the judge, "the statutes are not clear. Arabus has no certificate of manumission. This little pickaninny's word is certainly not to be trusted. My client is a respectable Christian

168

white man. Surely you will return his legal property to him."

"Mr. Chauncy, the only documents I see tell me that Ivers sent Arabus to fight for the nation's freedom— and by law he couldn't do that without freeing him first. Clearly Arabus is a free man. As for the girl—" Captain Ivers stomped his foot and banged his fist on the bench.

"Damn the whole lot of you!" Ivers said, and turned around and stomped out. Nobody said a thing for a minute. Then Mr. Wadsworth leaned over the bench and said, "Mr. Chauncy, it looks like you've lost a client. Mr. Goodrich, I see no reason to hold the girl. You prepare a certificate for me to sign. She's paid a heavy price for her freedom. Let's see that she doesn't lose it again."

I nearly busted out crying again, but Uncle Jack had such a big smile across his face that I just started laughing instead.

14

So that's what happened. Uncle Jack and me went off to Mr. Goodrich's house and had a little celebration. Then Uncle Jack went back to Stratford. It was his plan to get a little dory and set himself up in the fishing business and try to save enough money to buy Aunt Betsy and Dan free. It wasn't going to be easy, though; it would take a good while to collect up that much money. But he was bound to do it, and I figured he would.

But of course I sure didn't want to go back to Stratford. There was only one place I wanted to be: That was back down at Fraunces Tavern in New York.

It had something to do with the argumentative way I was sometimes. I'd got it figured out that being argumentative was the same as being free. I mean, if somebody could boss you around, you wasn't free, and that's why I was argumentative, because there was always somebody trying to boss me around. I hated having somebody over me, and I don't guess I was any different from anybody else. I mean the whole war, that had got my Ma and Pa killed, was just to keep the British from being over the Americans. And I could see that people had a mighty strong feeling for being free, if they was willing to risk being shot for it. So that was why I wanted to go down to New York. There was more of a chance of doing what I wanted to do there.

Of course, some people was going to be more free than others. There wasn't no way around that. Slaves wasn't going to be no freer under the Americans than they was under the British, and women was still going to have to keep to their place. I was black, and I was a woman, and I knew there was limits. But I could see that nobody was free all the way. There wasn't nobody who could do anything he wanted—not even Captain Ivers, nor Mr. Goodrich, nor Mr. Fraunces, nor anybody. Captain Ivers couldn't keep me and Uncle Jack in slavery; and Mr. Fraunces, he had to do what his customers wanted; and Mr. Goodrich took his orders from the judge; and the judge—well, I didn't know what his limit was, but I reckoned he had one. They was all stuck one way or another. It was just that some people was way down at the bottom of the heap and a lot more stuck than others. And if I went to New York and learned about taverns and such, maybe

172

someday I could have a tavern of my own. Oh, there was a chance that I couldn't, neither. But it was worth trying.

So Mr. Goodrich fixed it with a friend of his for me to work my way down to the city, and I went. They put me to work scrubbing the deck; but as the sloop pulled out of the New Haven harbor I stood up and watched the houses sink down as we sailed away. For I knew I wasn't just saying good-bye to Connecticut. A whole part of my life was over now. I was grown-up; and it was all going to be new.

How Much of
This Book Is True?

THE STORY OF JACK ARABUS, as we have told it in this book, is basically a true one. We have invented the details, of course, but Jack Arabus did exist and did fight with Washington's troops as we have told in the story. Upon his discharge, his former owner, Captain Thomas Ivers, attempted to return him to slavery. He ran away and was jailed, but successfully sued for his freedom, about as we have described it. The case is known as *Arabus v. Ivers,* and you can read the official account of it in the *Connecticut Reports* of trials. That one case guaranteed the freedom of about three hundred Connecticut Negroes who fought in the American Revolution.

The story of Black Sam Fraunces and his famous tavern is also essentially true. During the British occupation of New York, the tavern was renamed The Queen's Head and was a favorite inn for British officers. It got its old name back after the war, and has existed under that name more or less continuously until today. The tavern burned down twice, and we are not sure what the original building looked like. However, the present building on the original spot is a good replica of the sort of building that was used for taverns in those days. There is a museum there, as well as a restaurant, and you can visit it sometime if you are in New York City.

Black Sam Fraunces was a somewhat mysterious character. He was born in the West Indies, went to New York, and became a respected businessman there. Even though he was called Black Sam, we are not sure whether he was in fact black. On the New York census report of 1790 he is listed as white. It is our best guess that he was at least part black. But we cannot be sure of this.

We are not exactly sure what role he played in the war, either. He was certainly allowed by the British to continue to operate his tavern. But also during the war he was victualler for American troops, supplying food to encampments outside New York City. After the war President Washington hired him as steward of his household. He must certainly have been sympathetic to the rebel cause, and perhaps was spying for Washington.

The general background as we have given it here is also as accurate as we could make it. Whaleboat

176

raids on Long Island Sound of the kind we have Willy caught up in were common. Canvas Town was a real place and was as we have described it. In particular, the story of the massacre at Fort Griswold is taken from eye-witness accounts of the time. In fact, the inhumanity there was much worse than we describe it here. We found the events inside the Fort so gruesome that we could not describe them in print. There is a replica of Fort Griswold in Groton, which you can see if you are ever in that part of Connecticut.

Uncle Jack Arabus, Captain Ivers, Sam Fraunces, Mr. Goodrich, Mr. Chauncy, and Judge Wadsworth and Willy's Pa, Jordan Freeman, were real people. But the other main characters in this story are made up. Willy, Horace, Willy's Ma, Aunt Betsy, and Daniel and the rest are fictional. We have tried to make them as much like people of that day were, but it is always difficult for even the most careful historians to know exactly how things were in another time.

The language used in this book is a case in point. It is almost certainly not how people spoke at that time, for the reason that nobody knows how they spoke. We know how they wrote, because we have their diaries and letters, but of course the spoken language perishes with the times. We have therefore tried to give something of the flavor of how an uneducated black person might have spoken then. In truth, Willy's way of expressing herself is much too modern for the times, but once again we cannot be sure. We are more sure about the attitudes that Willy and others around her

177

had—the idea that women were inferior to men, blacks to whites, children to adults. Almost all historians agree that such ideas were held by nearly all Americans of the Revolutionary era.

In particular, we had to consider very carefully our use of the word *nigger*. This term is offensive to modern readers, and we certainly do not intend to be insulting. But it was commonly used in America right into the twentieth century, and it would have been a distortion of history to avoid its use entirely.

In sum, what we have tried to do in this book is give you something of the feeling of how life was lived in those days, and how it felt to be somebody like Willy or Horace, or Jack Arabus. And if you want to know if Jack was ever able to buy the freedom of Aunt Betsy and little Dan, you can read another book we wrote, *Jump Ship to Freedom.*

About the Authors

James Lincoln Collier is the coauthor, with his brother Christopher Collier, of the Newbery Honor Book *My Brother Sam Is Dead, The Bloody Country, The Winter Hero,* and *Jump Ship to Freedom.* He has written many other highly acclaimed books for young readers including *The Teddy Bear Habit* and, for adults, *The Making of Jazz.* He lives in New York City.

Christopher Collier is a professor of history at the University of Bridgeport in Connecticut. His field is early American history, especially the American Revolution. He is the author of *Roger Sherman's Connecticut: Yankee Politics and the American Revolution* and other works. He and his family live in Orange, Connecticut.